Lexie peeked o... see an empty ...

There were few pla... but Lexie waited in the doorway as Shaun checked the bathroom and closet.

"It is safe? Can I come in?" Whether she wanted to come in was another question entirely. Shaun hadn't told her the whole truth about himself, that much had become clear. But could she blame him? It wasn't as though she'd asked the right questions. Or any questions at all.

"All clear," he called. The sound of a sliding shower curtain was followed by his reappearance. "You'd better check if anything was taken, though. You're sure you locked the door when you left the room?"

Lexie's wide eyes narrowed and she crossed her arms, bristling at the implication. "Of course I did. You were standing right next to me and watched me do it."

He shrugged. "It doesn't make sense that someone would break into your room and not touch anything—"

Lexie crossed the room as he spoke. She lifted her bags off the bed—and screamed.

Michelle Karl is an unabashed bibliophile and romantic suspense author. She lives in Canada with her husband and an assortment of critters, including a codependent cat, an albino rabbit and an opinionated parrot. When she's not reading and consuming copious amounts of coffee, she writes the stories she'd like to find in her "to be read" pile. She also loves animals, world music and eating the last piece of cheesecake.

Books by Michelle Karl

Love Inspired Suspense

Fatal Freeze

FATAL FREEZE

MICHELLE KARL

HARLEQUIN® LOVE INSPIRED® SUSPENSE

Recycling programs
for this product may
not exist in your area.

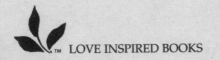
LOVE INSPIRED BOOKS

ISBN-13: 978-0-373-67676-7

Fatal Freeze

www.Harlequin.com

Printed in U.S.A.

And we know that all things work together for good
to them that love God, to them who are the called
according to His purpose.
                    –Romans 8:28

To Amy and Alley
Thanks for brainstorming with me at lunch that one time
And for all the pantry snacks

ONE

Lexie Reilly gave her car a final once-over, satisfied tYhat she hadn't forgotten anything for the sixteen-hour overnight ferry crossing to Newfoundland. She slung her travel bag and purse over her shoulder and pressed the car remote's lock button twice. The click-beep of the lock and alarm mechanism echoed back at her, and she noted with surprise that she stood alone on the car deck. Everyone else had already cleared out, leaving her amidst a sea of parked vehicles. The radio program she'd been listening to must have been more engaging than she'd realized.

Lexie frowned, feeling slightly uneasy. Aside from the rumble of the ship, it felt too quiet. No, too still. *Trust your instincts,* she thought. Where were the deck attendees? If she was being honest with herself, her instincts were telling her to get up to the passenger decks, find a cup of hot tea and get back to examining her file on Maria, the missing young woman she'd been searching for these past few months. She had clues to piece together before they docked in Argentia, New-foundland's historic port town and former United States military base.

Despite the ferry's protection against the early March air, Lexie shivered, looking forward to the warm lounge above. Her footsteps clanged as she walked alongside the cars, weaving through them to get to the stairs. As she crossed between a tall blue van and an oversize SUV, arms circled around her neck and waist, pinning her from behind.

"You shouldn't have come here," a scratchy, masculine voice growled.

Lexie tried to scream, but the pressure on her neck made it hard to breathe. She gasped for air and lifted her boot to stamp on his foot. He squeezed tighter, and tears streamed down Lexie's face as sparks flew in her vision. Every movement she made only increased the pressure on her throat. In moments, she would pass out, or worse. As Lexie's vision turned blurry, she thought she heard something—like shouting, from far away. Pounding footsteps came toward her and, as quickly as she'd been grabbed, her attacker released his grip, shoving her forward.

Lexie tumbled to the floor, gasping for air. Pain shot through her limbs with each breath, and she could still feel where the man's arm had pressed against her windpipe.

The footsteps stopped as they came close, and she sensed a presence beside her. A gentle touch on her shoulder sent waves of relief flooding through the pain. "Steady," said a calm male voice. "Are you all right? Do you need medical attention?"

Did she? Lexie squinted through the haze in her vision. She'd feel a whole lot better if someone had taken off after the attacker. He might still be caught, but this man in front of her would have to get moving.

"Go," she tried to croak, but it sounded more like a raspy gasp than an intelligible word.

"Let's get you to the upper deck," he said. An arm snaked around her back to rest under her shoulders. She tried to push his arm away and gesture in the general direction of her attacker's escape, but either her signaling skills needed some serious work, or this man was less motivated than he should have been to catch a criminal.

Lexie leaned against the nearest tire and squeezed her eyes shut. Her head and heart pounded. Had the attacker truly known who she was, and why she'd boarded the ferry? The warning had been unspecific, and he could have mistaken her for someone else—the lighting in the car deck made the whole area appear gray and muddled.

If anything, the attacker's threat only made her more determined to get to Newfoundland. Until now, she'd had no possible evidence that Maria's disappearance was anything more than another case of "runaway teenager." Maria's parents were convinced their daughter had skipped town out of anger after they'd forbidden her to spend time with a boy she'd been sweet on—but unlike most of Lexie's clients, Lexie had actually met Maria in person before. Lexie occasionally volunteered to drive the local youth group to their community events, and Maria had always come across as one of the most level-headed young adults among the group. On the other hand, she'd spent the drive to the ferry dock questioning how well she'd known the girl after all. Lexie hadn't even realized Maria was seeing anyone. Not that they'd had any deep conversations about life, but the whole situation hit far too close to home. For Maria's family's sake, Lexie would figure this out, no matter how long it took.

As for the man crouched in front of her, asking over and over if she needed medical attention... she could barely hear her own thoughts over his repeated questioning. When she finally shook her head in response, he took her left hand and turned it over, uncurling her fingers.

"Your palm is bleeding," he said. He traced gentle fingers around the scraped and dirtied base of her palm. "I'm going to call for medical assistance. The emergency phone is five feet away from us on the wall by the stairs. I'll be able to see you. You're safe."

I know I'm safe, and it's not because of you. "Fine," she rasped. The effort brought on a fit of coughing, which did nothing to ease the throb in her throat. It was ridiculous, sitting here. She had serious work to do, and only sixteen hours to do it in. "But I don't need a doctor. Just need to get to the upper deck."

The man huffed in frustration and stood. Moments later, Lexie heard him phoning for medical assistance. To her surprise, he didn't explain on the phone why she needed help, but told them to bring a first aid kit and a few extra, oddly specific, supplies. She didn't need an ophthalmoscope or penlight or whatever—a bit of iodine and a small bandage and she'd be fine.

Lexie braced against the car at her back and pushed upward, placing her hands on the hood for a few moments to catch her balance. Using one hand on the car for support, she reached to pick up her purse and travel bag from where they'd fallen.

"A medical team will be here in a minute," the man said, hanging up the phone and coming toward her. "Sit back down. They'll check to make sure no serious damage was done to your throat, since—"

"I'm fine, thank you." Lexie managed to lift her head to make eye contact with the man who'd come to her rescue. Her heart leaped into her throat as every muscle in her shoulders tensed. The man wore a red plaid shirt, a puffy black winter vest, jeans and a red knit toque. He looked like a lumberjack—or someone trying really hard to look like a lumberjack. Except that she knew him, or she had, eight years ago, and he definitely hadn't been lumberjack material.

In fact, the man in front of her was her own missing sister's former beau, looking as gorgeous as he did the day he broke Nikki's heart and sent her into a downward spiral...a spiral that led to Nikki's kidnapping almost eight years ago, only months after they'd met.

What were the chances she'd end up here and now, being rescued by *him*?

Shaun Carver blinked in surprise at the piercing hazel eyes that glared at him in fury. Eight years separated the last time they'd met, and she looked good.

Really, really good. She had longer hair than he remembered, and a maturity about her that replaced the teenage awkwardness of all those years ago. "Alexandra?" He extended his hand for a proper greeting, but she shook her head and hoisted her bags farther onto one shoulder. "Is that really you? Nicola's sister, right?"

Instead of acknowledging his question, she mumbled an incoherent phrase under her breath and broke eye contact. "I can take it from here, Carver."

Hearing his real name jolted Shaun out of the moment of incredulity and back to reality. "Just Shaun these days," he said, glad that they were the only people within earshot. He'd boarded the ferry under an alias, and there'd be a heap of trouble if the wrong people overheard and figured out his true purpose aboard the vessel. He doubted the CIA would appreciate him blowing his cover on a three-year, multi-continent human-trafficking operation thanks to an unexpected reunion with the little sister of a girl he'd briefly been friends with years ago.

"Whatever," she said, waving a dismissive hand. "Did you get a good look at his face? I need to report the incident to ship security. It would help to have a description."

Shaun shook his head. "Ski mask, wide shoulders. That's about it. His head and body were covered in black gear, so there's not much to go on. He had a distinctive gait —jerky but quick—so that might help, but I can take care of it. I saw the guy and can describe the incident. No need for you to relive it if you don't have to. Let's have the medical team look you over so you can enjoy the rest of the trip."

"You're joking, right?" Her eyes widened as her strained voice rose in volume. Their eyes met again, and Shaun was struck by the pang of familiarity. What he wouldn't give to have bumped into her at another time and place. On several occasions throughout the years, he'd wondered how Alexandra and Nicola were doing, but had never felt comfortable reaching out. He'd met the Reilly sisters on a youth mission trip to Botswana, and he'd quickly become friends with Nicola, both of them young and self-centered and eager to do anything but the volunteer work they'd come to Africa for. At the time, he'd had no idea that Nicola expected more than friendship from him, and it hadn't ended well once she made her intentions clear.

Alexandra continued to stare at him. "Someone tried to strangle me, and I shouldn't be worried?"

She crossed the distance between them, her steps sure and confident. He bristled at the intrusion into his personal space, but their difference in height made it seem as though he was being stalked by a kitten. She poked a finger toward his chest but stopped short of making contact. Shaun bit down on the inside of his cheek to stop himself from grinning. The kitten had claws. He'd never seen this side of the younger Reilly sister before.

"I don't know who you think you are, but you're mistaken if you assume I'm going to let this go. I have very important work to do, and while I appreciate your assistance, I can take it from here."

Important work? Now they were getting somewhere. "What kind of work, exactly? What have you been up to, Alexandra?"

Before she had a chance to respond, two medical staff in navy blue uniforms emerged from the stairwell, medical bags in their hands. Alexandra followed his gaze and actually growled before sighing in resignation. It was adorable, a fact that Shaun wisely kept to himself.

To his relief, she consented to being checked over, though she glared at him the entire time. He had arrested criminals who were less antagonistic toward him than she. Her attitude was baffling. He recalled Alexandra giving him the cold shoulder after he'd rebuffed Nicola's advances near the end of the mission trip, but that was eight years ago.

He remembered that trip as though it had been yesterday. As they'd spent time helping build a school and dig wells for impoverished families, Shaun had experienced a profound change in how he saw the world, discovering that he wanted to spend his life serving and protecting those in need. Attention-seeking party girl Nicola was a fun friend, sure, but he'd quickly realized he had no interest in pursuing a romantic relationship with her. Nicola had been angry when he'd told her he wasn't interested in dating, and she'd shocked him by demanding he never speak to her or her family again. He'd respected her wishes, and applied to the CIA's training program the following year. But now Alexandra stood in front of him, needing help. How could he say no?

When the medical team finished checking her over, and before she could request to talk with security, he strode forward. "I'll take her upstairs," he said, speaking over her protests. "Maybe it'll give us a chance to catch up."

He noted her crossed arms and downturned lips with interest. She'd grown into her beauty, with strong features that somehow remained delicately feminine—a stark contrast from her wispy, blonde sister. Or at least what he remembered of her sister. He hadn't seen either of them for nearly a decade.

"How've you been, Alexandra? Your sister's not here with you, is she?"

"It's Lexie," she said, gathering up her bags. "And no, of course she's not."

Had the Reilly girls had a falling out? "That's too bad. I'd have liked to have said hello." He couldn't quite read the look on Alexandra's—no, Lexie's—face. Confusion? Anger? "That's no reason *we* can't catch up, right?"

He shouldn't, though. He had an assignment to focus on, and yet…the attack, combined with her comment about important work, intrigued him. Gathering information was part of a CIA agent's job description, after all.

"You've got a lot of nerve, Carver," she said, turning back to the medical staff, who were re-packing their equipment. He winced, hearing her say his last name. How had she remembered it all this time? He needed to correct her privately, or else things could get more complicated than they already were. "I'd like to speak with security, please. They'll want to know about the incident here, for the safety of the passengers. I'll be up-stairs in the lounge. I'll try to sit near these stairs so that I'm easy to find."

The staff assured her they'd bring someone over and offered to escort her up to the lounge on the way. Without another word, Lexie followed them up several flights of stairs before being directed to turn left toward the lounge area at the front of the ship. Shaun followed behind, despite Lexie's obviously deliberate effort not to acknowledge his presence.

They emerged into a wide, open room, with enormous plate-glass windows that curved around the front of the ship. He would have to take advan-tage of the view at some point, but from where he stood at the entrance to the room, the only thing visible outside was a gray, fully clouded sky. What Shaun wouldn't give for a day or two of sunshine, like they'd had earlier in the week. This winter had been far too cold, the temperatures dipping and rising without warning, freezing melted snow into thick, slick ice that coated everything. He had been surprised to learn that the ferry would be making the three hundred and forty mile ocean journey today, considering the plunge into deep freeze last night.

Lexie sank into an empty seat a few feet from the door. Shaun followed and sat next to her as she placed her bags on the floor. She opened her travel bag and pulled out a red manila folder, tensing at his nearness as she placed it on her lap. Lexie stared straight ahead at the small coffee table by their feet.

"I'll talk to security for you," he said, despite her refusal to acknowledge him. "Trust me on this one. Let it go."

Lexie tapped an unpainted fingernail on the folder. "Trust you? That's rich." Her tone turned bitter. "Don't think I didn't notice your lack of urgency in pursuing the bad guy. Now there's someone aboard who might pose a danger to other passengers on the ship, and it sounds as if you're trying to threaten me to keep me from telling someone else about the incident, so, no. I'm not going to trust you just because you asked me to. Among other reasons."

It was a shot straight to the gut. What had he

done to become the bad guy? "My apologies. You're absolutely right. It's been a while and I suppose trust is something to be earned after all these years." He paused and considered his next words carefully. If her assailant meant to seriously harm her, she could place herself in danger again if she wasn't careful. "I'd hoped that stopping an attempt on your life, whatever the reason, would be worthy enough to gain trust."

Telling her why she needed to trust him would make this so much easier, but Shaun needed to protect his mission. He'd boarded the ferry on an anonymous tip to CIA headquarters that suggested there might be ties in Argentia to the human trafficking ring the CIA had been trying to bust for the past three years. Shaun was so close to cutting off the head of the snake, he could taste it. He'd bring the Wolf and his organization down, no matter the cost.

Shaun blinked as memory took shape. Nicola and Alexandra, disembarking from the Youth-Builders' bus in a dusty town in Botswana. *Hi, I'm Alexandra,* the brunette had said, *and this is my sister, Nicola. We came with the Canadian group. Where are you from?*

"Sorry," Lexie said, cutting through the strangely vivid memories. She looked startled by his honest appeal. "It's just that until fifteen minutes ago, I thought I had a straightforward job to do. Now I'm not so sure."

Now they were getting somewhere. "Maybe I can help." Lexie made no effort to hide the surprise on her face. "No, really. Tell me, what's the work you're doing, exactly?" He inclined his head toward the red folder. Her fingers flicked across its edge in impatience as she contemplated his offer of help.

Silence stretched like a rubber band until her gaze grew hard and distant, and she shook her head. "I can't. Client confidentiality. I…I've probably said too much already."

This made him pause. He'd have to tread with care and draw her out by reassuring her that she could trust him. Telling her everything would blow his cover, but maybe he could offer up a partial truth in hope she'd reciprocate with an exchange of information. If that attack had been deliberate, he needed to know.

"I promise you, I'm not involved. Not the way you're thinking, anyway. It's complicated, so trust me when I say you need to stay out of this. Let me handle it."

She rolled her eyes, making no effort to hide her frustration. Her limbs were locked tight against her small body, as though he had a contagious disease. The hostility astounded him, especially considering he'd saved her from a potentially life-threatening situation. "It's been a long time, Lexie. How've you been? What have you been up to?"

"You ask a lot of questions, Carver," she snapped. "You a cop? Got a badge to show me?"

Shaun rubbed his jaw. He needed to stop her from using his name. "It's Lane. Shaun Lane."

She arched a delicate eyebrow. "Is it now? I have a good memory for these kinds of things."

He swallowed hard. He'd faced down terrorists and real-life villains without so much as a flinch. Why did Lexie's observations bring a lump to his throat? "We all make changes. I got your name wrong, didn't I?"

"A shorter version of a long first name is a little different than an entirely new last name."

He needed to move this along before she started asking questions he couldn't answer. "Look, I work for…the government, and let's leave it at that. What about you? I'm getting a PI vibe, but I suspect that's not right, either."

A hint of a wry smile touched her lips. "No. I'm the vice president and a support counselor for a volunteer missing-persons organization."

Her shoulders dropped, and Shaun couldn't help but notice the purple bruise forming across her throat. "Hey, are you actually okay? That looks painful."

Lexie lifted pale fingers to the bruise, wincing at the touch. A small silver name bracelet slid from her wrist to her forearm. Shaun could just make out the engraving as the setting sunlight glinted off the name plate. Nikki.

"I'll be fine. I'm alive, and that's what matters."

Silence returned for a moment as Shaun churned over what to say next that wouldn't shut her down further. Lexie seemed to come to a decision when he didn't press her for more information. "The organization is named Lead Me Home National. We search for missing persons in Canada that law enforcement like the local police or even Interpol have given up on, or who aren't considered 'missing' for whatever reason. Or the family might fear going to the police, maybe because they or the family member entered the country illegally, that kind of thing. I'm searching for a girl named Maria who disappeared a few months ago."

Shaun's heart sank. "You aid and abet illegal immigrants?"

Lexie lifted the folder and slammed it down on her lap, fire blazing in her eyes. "No. It's a matter of human rights. Of everyone's right to have someone looking out for them, even when everyone else has given up, even when..."

Her voice trailed off, hitching on her words. The fierceness in her eyes had been replaced by a red-rimmed sadness, which she was trying unsuccessfully to blink away. Shaun laid his hand on her shoulder and mentally kicked himself.

Everyone dealt with trauma differently, and clearly the events of the past hour had brought something painful to the forefront.

"Sorry, I didn't mean to upset you." He scanned the room, desperate for a way to prevent her tears from flowing. He'd been the cause of too many tears in the distant and recent past, thanks to this job. Learning how to balance relationships and job requirements was a steeper learning curve than he'd ever expected. In a way, it had been easier before he'd realized how much he longed to share his life in a deep, committed relationship with someone who understood his drive to help and protect others.

Shaun's gaze landed on the coffee bar in the center of the room, where baristas handed out drinks and pastries to the waiting customers. He turned his attention back to Lexie, who was staring at his hand where it rested on her shoulder.

"Uh, I..." Shaun pulled his hand away and stood. "Can I get you a coffee? You look like you could use the caffeine."

Pink rose in her cheeks. "One cream, please."

At the coffee bar, Shaun kept his attention split between his place in line and Lexie. His stomach churned with frustration, and he found he couldn't keep his eyes off her. She'd be much safer if she stayed put and allowed him to do the searching for her attacker. It'd be foolish to encourage an unarmed woman to take on an opponent who'd just proven himself physically stronger than she.

Besides, he had his own search to conduct, and the people *he'd* come to search for were far more dangerous than a random man in a ski mask. Still, the coincidence made him pause. Here was a woman also searching for a missing person, and she'd been the victim of an attack. Could there be a connection?

Whether there was or not, a civilian nosing around for any reason might get herself hurt— she'd *already* gotten herself hurt. It could be worse, next time. Lexie's interference might also compromise his plans and destroy three years of painstaking intel and recon, putting the lives of those in the ring's clutches in further danger.

And while he understood God would forgive him if he messed this one up, he knew he would never, ever, forgive himself.

TWO

Lexie stared at the photo of Maria, but her real focus was elsewhere. She could barely believe it—she hadn't seen Shaun Carver for nearly a decade. She'd been sixteen years old when they'd first met, and he had been the hottest guy on the YouthBuilders' mission trip to Botswana—and he'd known it, too. She'd disliked him the moment they met, but not because she hadn't been attracted to him. It was because her sister *had* been, despite the point of the trip being to build a school for the local orphanage, not finding a future husband among the mission team. But when had Nikki ever done what she was supposed to?

She'd recognized him instantly on the parking deck, despite the strange lumberjack getup. He looked just as handsome as the day he'd broken her sister's heart. Shattered it to a million pieces is how Nikki had phrased it. What kind of guy would be so cruel as to lead a girl on, promising her the world and then dumping her the minute things got "complicated"? At least he'd recognized her, too, so he'd understand why she might be less than thrilled to see him. If she'd known he would be on this ferry, she'd have waited for the next boat.

What she really didn't understand was why he'd been acting so cheerful and laissez-faire about bumping into her after all this time. Could he really be so clueless? Did he honestly have no idea what he'd done? His cruelty had sent Nikki into the arms of a rebound boyfriend, a guy who'd clearly been a terrible influence and only encouraged her reckless personality…resulting in her disappearance. Or as Lexie believed, her kidnapping. It would have been easier to ignore Shaun and walk away when he'd asked about her work, but memories of Nikki had bubbled to the surface and she'd barely shut them down in time. Working on Maria's case felt too close to home at times, but it was getting easier to shove her grief aside—after all, it had been eight years since Nikki's disappearance. Lexie figured it was about time.

Lexie needed focus, because without it, another girl might very well disappear forever. Maria had already been missing for three months, and the longer it took to find her, the less likely she'd be found at all. While Maria's parents believed the girl had run away, Lexie had seen Maria's dress for her prom next month. According to her parents, Maria had saved up her earnings for a year to afford the five-hundred-dollar dream dress for the event. What kind of teenager would willingly give that up after working so hard for it?

It was tough enough to search for missing people when giving it her full focus, but having Shaun Carver—sorry, *Lane*—around provided an unwanted level of complication. A government lackey? Please. Guys like him were nothing but nosy, brawny wannabe heroes.

She glanced over her shoulder at him and shook her head. Shaun knelt on the floor, helping a young mother cram hundreds of spilled plastic blocks back into a cloth bag. The woman's toddler wasn't doing either of them any favors, grabbing pieces off the floor and throwing them at bemused passersby. Shaun and Lexie's coffees sat abandoned on the edge of an empty table. Okay, maybe he wasn't all bad. It *had* been nearly a decade since he'd callously dumped Nikki at the end of the trip. People could change, right?

Lexie sighed and turned her attention to the fading light through the window. Why did life have to be so complicated? Now was not the time or place for a walk down memory lane, despite Shaun's earlier eagerness for it. Getting him out of her business had to be the first priority or she'd get nothing done. If she could ditch Mr. Wannabe Superhero and investigate the attack on her own, maybe she could shove away the memories of Nikki for a little while longer.

She jumped at a sudden touch on her shoulder, but relief flooded through her body when a paper coffee cup with her name scrawled on the side crossed her field of vision. She took it and placed her folder on the coffee table. One seat over, Shaun took a sip from his own cup while scanning the room. He had a quiet strength about him, an air of confidence that made her want to trust him—despite the lumberjack outfit and his two-day scruff. That was new. At nineteen, but he'd kept his appearance immaculate, despite working in a dusty village in rural Africa. Nikki had found it appealing. Lexie had found it pretentious and ignorant. Now, it gave him a rugged handsomeness that made Lexie shift uncomfortably in her seat.

A stray curl of light brown hair escaped from underneath his toque, and Lexie resisted a sudden urge to lean forward and brush it out of his eyes. Shame blossomed in her belly. How could she even think that way, after how he'd hurt her sister? Heat stung her eyes, and Lexie blinked away another rising tide of memories and guilt. She needed to refocus on the job she'd come here to do. Her fingers tightened on the coffee cup, and she savored the sensation of fresh, hot coffee dancing across her tongue, heating her up from the inside. She held on to that, pulling her attention away from Shaun's searching gaze.

A few minutes later, two blue-uniformed ferry employees entered the lounge and scanned the room as though looking for someone. Before Lexie made the mental connection, Shaun had crossed the distance and ushered them out of the lounge and into the hallway. Security personnel! She tried to sit upright and push herself out of the chair, but her limbs felt heavy. She blinked, trying to clear a growing haze in her vision. The sounds around her grew muffled. Wasn't the coffee supposed to keep her—

"Lexie?"

Lexie's eyes fluttered open. She jerked up in her seat and stared at Shaun, whose look of concern had turned into a satisfied smirk. "What happened? I was about to follow you, but—"

"Need another coffee?" Shaun ran his fingers through his mop of hair, toque nowhere to be seen. "Though we should probably get you to your bunk. You can't sleep here overnight."

"It's not like I planned to do so." Had she been more tired than she'd realized? Lexie yawned and lifted her coffee cup from where she'd rested it between her hip and the chair. She raised the cup to take a sip, but set it down again in disappointment when no warmth radiated through the lid. A fresh cup would be nice, but she'd already accepted too much charity from someone who might as well be a stranger. Eight years was a long time. "It's okay, thanks. I want to do a little more thinking before I turn in for the night. And talk to security on my own. I can't believe you talked to them without me."

The smirk slipped, and he rubbed a hand across his jaw. "I thought you were following me to talk with them, honest. When I looked back and saw you weren't with us, I figured you'd changed your mind about letting me do the talking."

"I didn't plan to fall asleep. It was sudden. I just blacked out."

Shaun frowned. "Can I see your cup?" She handed it to him and he sniffed the contents. "No strange smell. You sure you're not just exhausted from what happened downstairs?"

"I wish you'd stop acting like I'm incapable of rational thought. You're the one who left the cups unattended while you cleaned up a toy spill. Maybe…maybe I was drugged. My name is on the cup here, plain as day."

"You're right." He rubbed his hand across his face. "But why would someone drug your coffee, Lexie?"

She rested her head against the back of her seat. "I don't know. It sounds crazy. And why me? I should call the police."

Shaun pulled a phone out of his pocket and

waved it at her. "The reception out here is terrible, and I've already talked to security. But if you're determined, I know exactly where the police station is in Argentia. I can show you the way once we dock."

She scowled at him, considering his offer. If he'd already talked to security, what good would her statement do? "Won't that be too late? The guy will have escaped by then."

"For all we know, he might have already jumped ship. But we'd cast off when I found you on the parking deck, and no one can survive more than a minute or two in ocean waters at these winter temperatures. Tell you what, we'll call the police station as soon as we get cell service back. Deal?"

It sounded reasonable. That way the ship could be locked down and searched before anyone disembarked. "Deal."

Shaun nodded and locked his fingers together, stretching his arms in front of him. "All right. Let's have a look at the folder, then. Maybe that contains some clues about why someone would go to the trouble of making sure you'd be asleep for a few minutes."

Lexie glanced at her lap and at the coffee table where Shaun's cup sat. "Don't you have it?"

Shaun shook his head and pointed at her bag. "Didn't you put it away when I brought the coffee over?"

Alarm bells rang in Lexie's head. "No, I thought I'd look through it when the caffeine kicked in. It was right here, I had my eye on it when you handed me the coffee." She refused to entertain the obvious notion before exploring all other possibilities.

She knelt on the floor and looked under the chairs and table, while Shaun stood and surveyed the area around them. They both came up empty-handed.

"It's gone," Lexie said, panic rising in her chest. "How can it be gone? I took a few sips and it sat right here, while you were—"

"Talking to security," he said in a flat voice. "I know you don't want to hear this, but someone may have come by and taken it. Best-case scenario, it was a passenger playing a prank, or someone mistook your folder for theirs."

He left the other option unspoken, but Lexie saw it in his eyes. He feared that the man who'd assaulted her had drugged her so he could steal it while she slept.

"All my notes are in there." Lexie groaned, reality setting in. "My photo of the girl I'm looking for, plus sensitive information on contacts."

Shaun frowned and scanned the room again. "You left a folder with sensitive information on a table? In a public area?"

"I didn't plan on falling asleep."

"I only walked away for a few minutes." He grimaced and ran his fingers through his hair. "Not good. Someone's watching you. Whatever information you have in that folder, it's important to them. Or they suspect it might be. Combined with the attack earlier, it seems like the situation is more serious than you thought. This girl might be in a lot of danger."

"I know." Lexie's voice carried across the room, and she felt her cheeks warm as several passengers turned to look at her. "I know," she continued, voice quieter. "But it's not like I expected someone to drug my coffee. It's not like I've done this before."

"Done what? Look for someone?" Shaun's eyebrows scrunched together as Lexie flopped back down into her chair. "I thought you said you worked for a missing-persons organization."

She nodded, feeling a weight in her chest. "I do. But I haven't tackled a search like this on my own before. I've spent several years proving I'm capable and trustworthy enough for a solo project, and now that I'm VP, I can't mess it up."

"Do you have a backup copy somewhere?"

Lexie shrugged. "I might be able to access some of it on my phone through email or cloud storage. The rest is on file at the office, which I could have someone scan and send to me." She dug through her bag for her phone, hope surging—until she looked at the reception icon in the upper right corner. Still no bars. "No signal, but you're right, I've had trouble getting decent reception for the past day or so. Maybe they haven't turned on the wireless yet?"

"I think they have an internet kiosk elsewhere on the ship." Shaun reached down and picked up her bags. "Let's find your room first. While you're getting set up, I'll find out where the kiosk is and then come back to walk you there. Sound like a plan?"

Sure, except for the part where he watched over her as though she was a china doll. "I'll be fine walking around on public decks. If whoever took the folder had wanted to hurt me, wouldn't they have done it then? Why go to all the trouble of potentially drugging my coffee?"

Shaun adjusted her bags on his shoulder. "Because the room was still full of other people. The coffee was likely a crime of opportunity—which we'll report as soon as we can. But if you happen to get lost down a corridor, or take a wrong turn and end up alone…" He shook his head when she tried to protest. "Maybe they only wanted the folder, sure. Maybe this is about something else. I can't answer that, I can only assess the risk—and the risk here is losing sight of the possibility that it might not have been an accident, or that having the information in your file will incite a reaction."

Lexie tried to come up with a reply that let him know how she felt about his insistence on trying to insert himself into a situation that didn't pertain to him, when a muffled, crunching noise interrupted everyone's conversations. The ship shuddered, and Lexie's heart leaped into her throat. "What was that?"

Around the room, worried faces searched for ferry staff, while many of the passengers in the room continued as they were. Before Lexie could ask Shaun if he knew anything, he'd already flagged down a passing attendant.

"Ice," he said, turning back to Lexie. "It's normal during winter months, but if we can hear the cracking, it means we're moving through a thick patch. The ship is fine."

Lexie noted that he looked back at the attendant a second time and followed his gaze. Several people in employee uniforms were making the rounds throughout the lounge, stopping to reassure passengers who demanded to know what they'd heard. Lexie crossed her seating area to look out the nearest window, but it had grown too dark outside to see anything.

And then Shaun was at her side, looking outside with her. Much to her annoyance, having him nearby felt comforting. She blamed it on the lure of familiarity. Definitely *not* attraction.

"Nature is unpredictable," he said. "But it's winter, so I guess they expect this kind of thing. It'll be fine. Let's get you to your cabin."

Lexie struggled for composure, not wanting to reveal just how scary the ship's shudder had been. Her brain knew how unlikely it was for a ship of this size to capsize—and as far as she knew, there'd never been a serious accident on this ferry crossing route—but her legs felt shaky as the crunching continued at random intervals. She didn't even have the strength to protest as Shaun touched her elbow and led her away from the window, escorting her through the ship's corridors to find the passenger cabins on the deck below.

The cabin deck hallways were narrow, providing just enough room for two people to pass each other or for a wheelchair to navigate successfully. At room forty-two, Lexie dug the key card out of her pocket and unlocked the door.

She'd reserved the smallest, most austere room they offered—the coach of ferry cabins—and the bunk bed on the left wall gave the place a college dorm feel. The rest of the room contained a desk and chair, a little bathroom and shower, and a window that overlooked the ocean. It was no Hilton Suites, but it would do for an overnight trip.

"Thanks," she said, when Shaun pushed past her to place her bags on the floor. "But you didn't need to carry those."

"It's nothing." He folded his arms and glanced

around the room. "Basic amenities? And I bet you fly coach, too."

"Of course. I'm being responsible with company funds. What's your point?"

He shrugged and exited the room, tapping on the door frame. "I bet your sister wouldn't go for this. If Nicola were here, she'd—"

Lexie's temper flared. How dare he even speak her name? "Because you're an expert on my family? Please, tell me more."

Shaun stepped back, his face a mask of confusion. "I was just suggesting—"

"Stop suggesting, then." If he hadn't lead her sister on and then broken her heart eight years ago, well, they wouldn't even be here right now.

"Fine." Shaun exhaled through his nose, clenching his jaw. "I'm going to go find out where the computers are. I recommend you stay here and lock the door. Don't open it to anyone except me. I'll knock twice, wait ten seconds, and then knock once."

Lexie stared at him. When had Shaun become a conspiracy nut? The guy had no idea how this kind of thing worked. "I don't see why I can't come with you."

"Safety," he said, his voice betraying a hint of annoyance.

"The only person in danger here is the girl I need to find. And I can't find her without the information from that folder." Did he really think she'd act carelessly after the events of the past hour?

Shaun raised his hands, the corners of his mouth turning down into a scowl. "Lexie, I need you to listen—"

Another crunching noise reverberated throughout the ship and Lexie put her hand on the wall to steady herself. The ship shuddered more violently this time, and the noise continued instead of quieting. Her heartbeat sped up, pounding in her ears.

"You think that's normal?" Lexie almost spat the words at Shaun, whose scowl had vanished, replaced by concern. "Pretty sure ferries aren't supposed to sound like a bag of chips when they sail."

He shook his head and caught her gaze. Lexie stopped the gasp that threatened escape. He was worried, and he wasn't trying to hide it. For some reason, that made her feel better. Despite their acquaintance being separated by almost a decade, a familiar face in a moment of uncertainty helped to quell her immediate panic.

"Keep the door closed. I'll be right back. Don't do anything rash."

She shut the door behind him, despite wanting to slam it in sudden anger at his parting comment. Who did he think he was, telling her not to do anything rash? He didn't know her. Or her sister. Not anymore, anyway, and he'd made it quite clear all those years ago that he didn't care to. Lexie sucked in a deep breath, trying to ease the tingle of adrenaline. The last thing she needed was to lose control of her emotions. She had a job to do, and if Shaun insisted on being a part of it, surely she could put up with an annoying hero-wannabe for a little while longer. He had potentially saved her life, after all. When she got the information from her folder back, she'd politely ask him to stop distracting her for the rest of the trip.

She sat on the bed and drew her knees up to her chest, feeling resolute, yet unable to shake the strangeness of Shaun's confused reaction to her words moments ago. This was not the time to dwell on it, though. She needed to focus, and Shaun would provide nothing but distraction.

So why did she feel a pang of regret at the thought of sending him away?

Shaun wandered through the ferry's halls, wincing at the unending crunch and jar of the ship. Worried faces peeked out of cabin doors, and there were fewer employees around than there had been a few minutes before. Had they all run off to find out what was happening? Hopefully, that meant there would be a ship-wide announcement to reassure the passengers before they started mobbing the captain's quarters. The thought of having Lexie's assailant amidst the mob of angry, scared passengers didn't sit well—it would provide the perfect cover for her to be injured, or worse.

The muscles in Shaun's neck tensed as he thought about Lexie's shock at losing her folder. Hadn't she been the more docile of the Reilly sisters? But now after less than an hour with her, it wouldn't surprise him if she'd left the room the moment he was out of sight. It was bizarre that they'd ended up on the same ship bound for the same place, but even stranger was Lexie's reaction to his question about her sister. He regretted not delving further into that immediately, but she'd reacted with such hostility that he'd let instinct take over and backed off.

Not exactly the mark of a superspy, allowing himself to be rattled by an attractive woman from his past. *Did* he find her attractive? Sure, in a platonic, purely aesthetic… Oh, who was he trying to convince, anyway? She'd been the cute little sister before, but now? She'd blossomed, all right. Lexie had gumption to be in the missing-persons business, too. They'd make a good team if he could manage to quell her hostility. Letting her in on the details of his assignment might do just that, but protecting his alias could get tricky. On a typical assignment, he needed to protect his identity at all costs, but she knew his full name and they shared a past—albeit through another person, but it might be enough for a mission-destroying slipup.

Bringing her in the loop, even a little, could help protect them both. He'd discuss it with HQ on his next check-in.

Shaun rounded a corner and saw a bank of computer cubicles through a set of glass doors at the end of the hall. He paused and had decided to go back to get Lexie when a scruffy employee in a white uniform pushed open one of the doors and strode toward him, purpose in his step.

"Excuse me," Shaun said, pasting a smile on his face. "Can you tell me what's happening with—" The employee shook his head in silence and brushed past Shaun without making eye contact.

"Excuse me?" Shaun raised his voice, staring after the employee. He wanted to give the man the benefit of the doubt—the ongoing noise was extremely worrisome—but it was no excuse to be rude. The man disappeared around the corner without another word. *Some people.* Shaun figured he might as well take a look inside the computer area to make sure the internet access was working.

All the chairs and computers were lined up in a row inside little library cubicles with instructional sheets tacked above the monitors. No, Shaun noted, not all the chairs. The final chair in the row sat slightly askew. His intuition urged him toward it.

Shaun sat and shook the mouse to wake up the screen. A sudden coldness hit his core.

Whomever had previously used this computer left in a hurry, because up on the screen—logged in, and with a list of files in clear view—was Lexie's cloud storage account. The coldness spread and chilled his spine as he noted another open tab. Lexie's email. He checked her account details, changed her password and logged out.

It had to be the same person. Lexie's attacker had been here minutes before. But what worried Shaun even more was that the attacker wasn't here now. And Lexie was alone.

THREE

Shaun thought of the employee he'd passed in the hallway. The man might have seen who had used the computer. In fact, he might have been in such a hurry because he'd been held back by a recent guest. If Shaun moved now, maybe he could catch him and get a description.

Shaun leaped up from the computer and raced through the glass doors, slowing his pace only when he reached the next hallway. He looked both ways, seeing several other people in white employee uniforms engaged by other guests. None looked familiar. The employee couldn't have gone too far, though. There were too many curious and worried passengers around to have made it far without being stopped to answer questions.

Excusing himself past groups of concerned faces, Shaun paced the corridors, scanning every hallway in both directions. The employee had vanished. After five minutes, Shaun had to admit he'd lost him. That made getting back to Lexie the next priority.

He'd have to tell her what he'd found, but maybe she'd be able to tell if the hacker had had time to read any of her documents. The room attendant had to come back eventually. Shaun would question him then, or find one of the security guys and learn whose responsibility it was to keep an eye on the computer room.

Shaun jogged down the stairs and hallways to get to Lexie's room. He followed the pattern of knocks and, to his relief, she opened the door the moment he finished the final knock. She appeared unimpressed as her face tilted up expectantly, jaw set in defiance, a fire blazing in her eyes that was betrayed by the quiver in the corner of her delicate mouth. A knot formed in Shaun's gut and he found himself suddenly conscious of how close she stood to him. He struggled to hold himself together, her vulnerability in the moment causing him to inexplicably yearn to hold her close and protect her from danger.

Lexie's emotions bubbled near the surface, about to spill over. It thrilled him. *Intrigued* him. His head screamed at him to run, that this pull toward her was ridiculous, but his feet remained firmly planted to the ground. What would she do if he pulled her into his arms and promised everything would be all right?

Lexie seemed to sense a shift in the air between them and stepped back. "You found something?"

He swallowed—*cool it, buddy*—and glanced both directions down the hall. "Yes, but you'd better come with me."

To his surprise, Lexie didn't hesitate. She stepped out of the room and locked it, no questions asked. She must have noticed his shock, because she raised one eyebrow and tilted her head. "What? You wanted me to try trusting you."

Warmth returned to his center, easing the cold that had come with learning someone had accessed her private files—but following that came the regret that he couldn't yet be honest about why he'd boarded the ferry. In his book, omission of information was as harmful as a lie. Would knowing the truth break her fragile trust? *God, give me strength.*

She followed him in silence to the computer room, where he led her to the last terminal. He brought up the webpage to log into her email with the new password he'd given her, then pulled out a chair so she could sit down.

Lexie stared in disbelief as her inbox loaded. "What…what's this? How'd you get into my email?" She looked up at him with accusation, but he shook his head and reached across, clicking open the other tab.

"I didn't, Lexie. But I have a good idea who did."

She sputtered half words, eyes glued to the screen. "Someone hacked my account? But that doesn't make any sense. Why would anyone want to read my messages?"

"Check if anything is missing. Whatever you had in that folder gave someone enough information to hack your email and your online storage account. They want to know what you know."

She swallowed hard and closed her eyes. "I've been meaning to change my passwords to something more secure. I've been using my dog's name. Easy to guess with a quick search on social media. Maybe we should call the police, have them meet us at the dock. They could dust this terminal for fingerprints or clues or something."

"I'd already touched it," Shaun said. "And do you really want to make this area an active crime scene? We'd have to cordon the room off and guests will ask questions. There's no way of being sure some kid or joker wouldn't tamper with the area, and I have a feeling security doesn't have enough manpower to post a guard outside."

Lexie scanned the contents of her accounts as Shaun paced the floor. Had someone been looking for additional, specific information? The more he thought about it, the more he grew certain that the same young woman Lexie was looking for had to be tied to the organization he hunted.

"Have we stopped moving?"

Shaun snapped out of his thoughts. Lexie jumped from her seat and jogged toward the doors at the same time as a blue-uniformed employee came toward them down the hallway. Shaun couldn't make out his face due to the way the hall lights reflected on the glass doors, but the employee appeared to be moving at a very brisk pace.

"Oh!" Lexie looked back over her shoulder. "I'll ask this guy. Maybe I'm wrong, but it seems like we've stopped. Don't you feel it?"

An uneasiness rose in Shaun's gut as the employee continued his approach, though Shaun couldn't pinpoint why. The way he moved seemed wrong, like he had something else in mind beyond attending the computer terminals.

The employee and Lexie reached the doors at the same time, Lexie still looking over her shoulder for an answer from Shaun. Shaun saw the man's hand disappear, as though reaching into his belt for something.

"Get away from there!" Shaun shouted and darted forward, ready to place himself in front of her as a human shield.

Lexie stopped, but the employee had already opened the door and stepped inside. He glanced between Shaun and Lexie and then over his shoulder, where a group of giggling teenage girls followed behind. "Is something wrong, sir?"

The tension in Shaun's shoulders refused to unclench. "I don't know. Is it?"

"Shaun?" Lexie looked between him and the employee. "What's going on?"

"Come over here," Shaun said, drawing his words out. "Toward me. Don't turn around."

The employee's eyes widened. "Sir?"

The teens pushed through the glass doors and into the room, laughing and whispering in each other's ears. Shaun's tension eased as the employee gestured to the terminals. "Here you are, ladies. Twenty minute maximum per session, please."

"Sorry," Shaun said, adding a brief laugh to diffuse the moment. "I thought you were someone else. I don't suppose you know if there's been anyone else in this room over the past hour or so, other than myself?"

The man shook his head, and Shaun finally pulled his observations away from the man's face to read the name tag. Josh.

"Sorry, sir. I've come from a briefing, myself." Josh divided his attention between Shaun and the teenagers. "Personnel are being shifted around at the moment."

"Do you know which staff member was stationed in this area on departure?"

Josh pulled on the edge of his shirt, straightening out a rogue wrinkle. "We don't typically station someone in this room for the duration of the trip. We have a few staff members with IT experience who check in every so often, but there's a call button at the back wall in case of any technical issues."

Shaun rubbed his chin, considering the best way to ask his question without alarming anyone. "Would you happen to know who's on the schedule to do the first round of checks tonight?"

Josh grinned and nodded. "Yes. That would be me, sir. Security does initial sweeps at departure, but Sheila has the bulk of the overnight run. I'm on call for this room until then."

"Did I see you down here earlier? Pass you in the hallway?"

Josh's smile disappeared. "No, that wasn't me. Sorry I can't be of more help."

Shaun gestured to Lexie, and she stepped closer to him as Josh vanished through a staff door. A physical attack, drugged coffee, stolen folder, hacked email and no leads. Complications would abound if he continued to exclude Lexie from his op, but she clearly had trust issues when it came to men. Or when it came to *him*, for some reason.

"I have a theory about your hacked email, but we can't talk about it here. We need either a public place with plenty of noise or a closed room where no one can overhear. Did you have enough time to see if anything is missing?"

Lexie frowned and looked between the bank of computers and the door. "Oh no, you don't. Mind telling me what that was about?"

"I will, as soon as we get somewhere that isn't full of listening ears." He inclined his head toward the teens, who were involved in an apparently hilarious game on a social networking website.

"Fine. Hang on a sec." Lexie crossed her arms and returned to the computer. She tapped on the keyboard a few times before turning off the screen. "We can talk in my cabin, but I'd like to pick up another coffee since I didn't get much out of that first one."

Shaun pressed his lips together. He wanted to get this conversation over with, but it would do no good if she stayed on the defensive. Maybe with another coffee and a snack, she'd be more amicable to discussing what had happened.

"All right, but let's make it quick."

She glanced at him over her shoulder, annoyance rippling through her features. "You don't have to follow me. The halls are full of people. I can meet you at my cabin."

Instead of responding, he shook his head and kept pace behind her. No use trying to convince her of the necessity of teamwork before he'd had a chance to explain.

"My case files were gone, by the way," she said as they descended the stairs to the deck below.

"Everything has been deleted. Somebody doesn't want me having access to information while I'm on board."

Lexie noticed Shaun startle and nearly miss the next step. He grabbed onto the railing to steady himself, but she didn't regret the tone of her delivery—these halls were full of passengers already worried about the sounds coming from outside the ship. Showing alarm would just add to the high tensions in the air.

They walked to the lounge in silence, where Lexie bought another cup of coffee and a bag of trail mix.

"You're sure stuff was deleted?" His voice was light and upbeat, following her cue as they made their way back to her room. "Just the files on the case or other things, too?"

"Just the case," she said, smiling as they passed a family of four in the hallway. The whole family wore fuzzy pajamas, and the two young children clutched plush toy characters from a recent animated film. The worried expressions on the parents' faces suggested that no one knew yet what was going on. Lexie wished they'd make an announcement, but the calmness of the staff was mildly reassuring. If the situation were serious, surely they'd be evacuating people by now. "In fact," Lexie continued, looking over her shoulder as they rounded the corner into her room's hallway, "I think—"

Without warning, Shaun jumped forward and flung his arm out in front of Lexie, grabbing her shoulder to push her behind him against the wall. She winced at the pain of being slammed against a hard surface, but gritted her teeth to stay silent.

Lexie followed Shaun's gaze to her doorway. It stood open about three inches, and though she'd intentionally left the light on before leaving for the computer room, no light shone through the door now.

"Stay here," Shaun whispered. He crept forward with slow, steady steps, but Lexie's attention was drawn to his right hand. He'd placed his hand inside his puffy vest, next to his right hip. There was only one reason a person would position their hand that way in a threatening situation, and it caused Lexie's heart to pound even faster.

Why is he armed? She had to say something. Even if he had a perfectly good explanation, drawing a concealed weapon on board a Canadian passenger ferry could send him straight to prison. "Shaun." Lexie's voice wavered, but he ignored her, moving toward the door. "Shaun?"

He stopped at the edge of her door, cocking his head to listen. He glanced back at her and gestured for her to move toward him. She stopped about three feet away and watched as Shaun, with the practiced grace of a professional, slid his back against the door and reached his left hand slowly through the crack. The light switch clicked on and Shaun simultaneously slammed his palm against the door, which flew open.

Lexie peeked over Shaun's shoulder to see an empty room. There were few places to hide in these small cabins, but Lexie waited in the doorway as Shaun checked the bathroom and closet.

"It is safe? Can I come in?" Whether she wanted to come in was another question entirely. Shaun hadn't told her the whole truth about himself, that much had become clear. But could she blame him? It wasn't as though she'd asked the right questions. Or any questions at all.

"All clear," he called. The sound of a sliding shower curtain was followed by his reappearance. "You'd better check if anything was taken, though. You're sure you locked the door when you left the room?"

Lexie's wide eyes narrowed and she crossed her arms, bristling at the implication. "Of course I did. You were standing right next to me and watched me do it."

He shrugged. "It doesn't make sense that someone would break into your room and not touch anything—"

Lexie crossed the room as he spoke. She lifted her bags off the bed—and screamed.

The bags tumbled from her hands and she stumbled backward, bumping into Shaun, who had moved across the room to grip her shoulders. An empty hollow formed in her stomach as tears sprang forth. She tried without success to blink them away.

Shaun's grip tightened as he followed her gaze to the center of her bunk. Behind Lexie's bags, someone had used a small, wood-handled hunting knife to spear the photo of Maria from the stolen folder to the bunk. Between the photo and the blade, a short braid of glossy black hair had been pinned to the image.

Lexie willed herself to step closer. There was writing on the bottom of the photo, which she didn't recall seeing before. "Shaun?" The effort to raise her voice above a whisper was too much, and the bruises along her throat began to throb from shock. Almost every time Lexie had seen Maria, the young woman had worn her hair in a beautiful long braid. This had to be hers. Someone had cut her hair. But *why*?

Shaun turned her to face him, forcing her attentions away from the photo and threatening knife. To her surprise, Shaun had a hint of a smile on his face. "Breathe, Lexie. I know this is beyond scary, but it's not as bad as it seems."

Fury rose in her gut. "Not as bad as it seems? What's wrong with you? I'm trying to find a girl who has either run away from home or had something horrible happen to her and now there's a lock of her *hair* on my bedspread—"

Shaun placed gentle hands on her cheeks, commanding focus. "Yes, it's terrible. But think about it this way. If that's Maria's hair? That means she's *on board this ship.*"

Lexie felt the blood drain from her face. She blinked against light-headedness, willing herself to focus on the man in front of her. "That means I can find her."

"*We* can find her," Shaun said, emphasizing the first word. "But there are a few things we need to talk about first. I'm going to call security and get them up here to secure the room."

She nodded, but her attention was drawn back to the photo. With her tears under control, she could now read what had been written at the bottom, in thick red paint. No, not paint. Lexie swallowed against the rising contents of her stomach as she read the two words smeared there: STOP SEARCHING.

"Or what?" Lexie whispered, glancing back at Shaun. "Do you think they'll hurt Maria?"

Shaun's shoulders drooped as he looked from the photo to Lexie. He scratched his chin and sighed in resignation. "No, Lexie. Think about it. Their target is *you*."

FOUR

Lexie sank into the closest chair, Shaun's deduction ringing in her ears. None of this made sense. Why target *her*? Sure, Lexie had her suspicions about Maria's disappearance, but she'd honestly thought that her parents would have received a ransom note or message by now. The lack of communication from an abductor or kidnapper had only reinforced Maria's parents' belief that their daughter had run away, and Lexie had had to follow clues and an anonymous tip that led her on this trip. But with Lexie's folder disappearing, the email hack and now the lopped-off braid and warning message, the whole thing spoke of something bigger going on. Had there been truth to Shaun's warning, after all?

He'd brought a gun on board, of that much she was certain, but it didn't explain his involvement or the reason why someone would try to scare her off what should be an innocuous retrieval of a mildly rebellious young woman. Or even if it did turn out to be kidnapping, why hadn't anyone asked for money? Lexie swallowed the urge to demand an explanation from Shaun. She'd get answers from him once the security team examined the strange mess on her bunk.

"I think," she began, striving to keep from staring at either the bunk or where she suspected the gun was tucked on Shaun's belt, "that you have some explaining to do." Before she could finish her thoughts, heat rushed from her belly to her forehead. A ringing in her ears drowned out Shaun's response. Her lungs seemed to decide that breathing was optional, and beads of sweat broke out along her forehead.

Shaun gripped her shoulders, his face blurry in her compromised vision. "Lexie? Stay with me, Lexie. What's wrong? Are you ill?"

Barely lucid, Lexie waved a limp arm toward the bathroom, hoping Shaun would get the message. He disappeared and returned with a plastic cup of water, which he tilted up to her lips. She drank, grateful for the cooling effect of the liquid, but beyond mortified that she'd lost the strength to hold the cup herself. She squeezed her eyes shut and let the panic attack run its course.

After a few minutes of labored breathing and intense internal waves of heat, Lexie felt well enough to open her eyes again. Shaun knelt in front of her chair, concern etched across his features. "What happened? Should I call a nurse?"

Lexie shook her head and downed the rest of the water. "Panic attack. I'm okay, I'll just feel a little dizzy for a few hours."

"You're sure you don't need medical attention? I can have one of the nurses down here in minutes."

Under different circumstances, Lexie might have laughed and explained the details of what a panic attack entailed, but right now she felt more annoyed with her body's bad timing and unpredictable response to stress than anything else. "No nurse needed, all right? This happens once in a while. It's not a condition I can control. It feels like I'm dying for about ten to fifteen minutes and then I'm fine."

Lexie wished her cabin had an extra room she could disappear into for a few minutes, not only to give her body a break from trying to process the stresses of the day, but also to get away from the clear worry on Shaun's face. His concern made her stomach queasy, mostly because it didn't make sense. How could someone who'd so callously shattered her sister's heart act with such tenderness?

Heat rose in her cheeks as she realized she'd been staring at him. He stared back, refusing to break eye contact. A gasp rose in her throat and she swallowed it down, looking away with effort. No, no, no. Shaun was all wrong for her.

She took a deep breath and tried to focus on the present. Someone had left her a warning, and she needed to know why. "The only reason I can think of for that message," she said, working it out as she spoke, "would be if Maria isn't simply missing, as her parents believe. Whoever did this means business. They have to know I'm looking for her, which only confirms the worst-case scenario. Shaun, Maria left her prom dress behind. It doesn't make sense."

"You're suggesting she might have been taken?" Weariness betrayed Shaun's otherwise confident demeanor. "Because you're on the right track, in that case."

Lexie shot him a sharp look. "You know about this? Let me guess—I should stay out of it and let you handle things."

Shaun ran his fingers through his hair and leaned against the desk. "I think we're beyond that. In brief, kidnapping isn't far off. The correct term here is likely trafficking, though I don't want to jump the gun just yet."

Lexie cringed at his choice of words. "Because anything to do with a handgun on Canadian soil would be problematic."

Shaun squinted at her. "Right."

Since he didn't rise to the bait, she pounced on

the rest of his know-it-all commentary. "And I don't see how trafficking fits into this. We're on a ferry to Newfoundland. Last time I heard about trafficking, it involved moving drugs or weapons across the Pacific."

"Exactly. Which would make the Atlantic an ideal route for a savvy trafficker with connections and the know-how to get their cargo from point A to B."

"Cargo? Their drugs?"

Shaun shook his head, crossing his arms over his chest. "I'm afraid not. It's far worse than that. There are groups around the world who traffic people, Lexie. They kidnap young women and sell them to the highest bidder for work in factories or as domestic help to people who have more money than brains or morals. These girls don't know what they're getting into, and are usually enticed by the promise of a great job in a flashy foreign country. They're offered high salaries and plenty of additional perks, but by the time the girls realize they've been duped, it's far too late."

Lexie's stomach churned as she tucked her knees up to her chin, wrapping her arms around her legs. "I thought that kind of thing only happened overseas, not here. I've wondered why the girls don't just run away, but I know it's much more complicated than that. It's hard to believe this goes on without the whole world freaking out about it."

Shaun sighed. "It's a harder problem to solve than it sounds. These people operate covertly, and yes, even here in North America. They're smart. And it's not unusual to drug these young women en route. By the time the girls get to the factory or new home, they're either threatened with bodily harm or their captors threaten to hurt the girls' families if they don't cooperate. So they go along with it, working themselves to the bone, while the factory owners reap excess profits from their cheaply made products."

It sounded insane, and yet…what other explanation could there be? The world made less sense by the minute. "How do you know all this?" she asked, peering up at him. He looked far too relaxed if what he'd just told her was true.

He pushed away from the desk and crossed the cabin to the emergency phone. "I'm going to call security, all right? They're going to want to deal with this before we make a mess of it."

Lexie unfurled her legs and stretched, hoping to work out the crick in her lower back from the earlier events of the day. Once security completed their sweep of the room, she and Shaun were going to have a serious talk, whether he liked it or not. He knew far too much to be a simple passenger on board the ship—not to mention the gun she was sure he had hidden in his waistband.

Shaun Lane had a secret, and she intended to figure it out.

Shaun's heart thudded as he replaced the phone receiver. It had become quite apparent that he needed to bring Lexie in on his case. The woman had a good head on her shoulders, and she wouldn't accept his diversions for long. He had to call his case officer with an update sometime in the next few hours anyway, and he needed to clarify how much he could tell Lexie about his search for the Wolf without leading her into even more danger.

On the other side of the room, Lexie's stare bore holes into his skull. He admired her persistence— and understood her desire for answers perhaps more than anyone else aboard—but safety had to come first. Whoever left the braid and the message knew very well who she searched for, but likely hadn't yet figured out Shaun's purpose here. That put her in the line of fire and left him with the option of sticking by her side for the next twelve hours or so until they docked…not that he'd complain about spending more time around her, but with it came the possibility of being distracted for entirely the wrong reasons.

As he contemplated what to say to ease her

raised hackles, crackling came through a speaker in the corner of the room.

"Ship-wide announcement?" Shaun watched as surprise flit across Lexie's visage. She already looked tired. Hopefully this announcement would bring some good news about the noises around the ship.

A pleasant, masculine voice with a heavy Newfoundland accent came over the speaker. "Good evening to all passengers of the *MV Providence*. This is your captain speaking, and on behalf of myself and the crew, we'd like to thank you for choosing Atlantic Voyages for your journey to Argentia this evening. No doubt you've heard quite the ruckus outside, and we'd like to ease your minds. Please rest assured, the ship is in no danger. It's quite natural for ice to form this time of year, though it's atypical for ice to reform this quickly and this thick after a warm spell. As you know, the weather this year has been a mite unpredictable. However, we are not, repeat *not*, going to sink."

The captain paused, and Shaun regarded Lexie. She'd taken his place leaning against the desk, her arms folded and hands tucked against her sides. An urge to cross the room and rub her shoulders for reassurance tugged at his gut, but she appeared less than welcome to any sort of interfering comfort at the moment.

"What sometimes happens," the captain continued, "is the ice thickens to the point where the ferry is unable to break through the ice on her own. We're also unable to turn around and return to harbor. But rest assured! An icebreaker from the Canadian Coast Guard is on its way."

Lexie glanced his direction, met his eyes and looked quickly away. What was she thinking? He'd give more than a penny for her thoughts. He'd pay a whole dollar—what was it they called them in Canada? Loonies?

"So, please sit tight and enjoy the ship's amenities. A special, complimentary evening buffet will be provided by our kitchen staff in about a half hour's time, and we'll provide hot beverages for the remainder of the evening at no cost. Current estimates put us docking into Argentia late tomorrow evening—a slight delay from our original estimated arrival time. We will continue to provide updates as the situation develops."

The speaker broadcast ended with a click. Shaun didn't even attempt to hide the sigh that welled up, releasing it in a long, drawn-out breath. Having the ferry trapped in ice presented an additional complication, namely that it meant more time in an enclosed vessel with someone who wanted to hurt Lexie. If his suspicions were correct, that someone also happened to be a notorious criminal who had eluded him for the past three years.

This left Shaun with just one option: Find the Wolf and take him into custody before he could hurt Lexie or anyone else. First things first, though. He had a question, the answer to which might provide some insight into the situation.

"The security team should be here in a minute," he said. "But before they get here, I'm curious. What made you pick this ferry? Specifically, I mean." He wasn't entirely sure where he was going with this, but his gut told him it might be important.

Lexie raised one eyebrow at him. "If you must know, though I don't think it's any of your business, we received an anonymous tip at Lead Me Home. The tipster saw Maria's photo on our website and called to tell us he saw someone matching her description at the last gas station on the highway before the ferry terminal. Logic followed that she might be headed to Newfoundland, as there isn't really anywhere else to go from here. And the small community of North Sydney, Nova Scotia, isn't the kind of place a person can run to in order to disappear. It's not unusual for us to get tips like this. Folks call in sightings of people we're searching for, or report whispers and rumors. Sometimes finding a person is as simple as a friend knowing where their buddy has gone for the weekend, or an employee at a rehab facility letting us know the person has checked in. This one came in about

Maria, so I followed it. I didn't pick this ship for any particular purpose, just got on the road as soon as I could after the tip came in."

Buzzers went off in Shaun's ears as he listened to Lexie's explanation. As a CIA operative, he relied on leads from anonymous sources on a regular basis, following up on promising tips and using the intel to assist sensitive investigations. The kicker here? He'd undertaken the voyage to Newfoundland for a similar reason, after receiving a tip that possible suspects with ties to the Wolf might be operating out of Argentia. It could be a coincidence, but in his experience, very few happenings in life could truly be chalked up to coincidence.

Had the same anonymous tipster provided intel to the CIA and to Lexie's missing-persons organization? It seemed unlikely and far-fetched, but then again, so did the fact that he'd bumped into Nicola's sister on a ferry to Newfoundland, far from both of their homes.

And even more bizarre? That Lexie might possibly be targeted by the same man he'd been trying to bring down for the past three years.

Although he stood on the other side of the room, Lexie felt keenly aware of Shaun's presence. His concern for her safety had softened the edges of her anger, though allowing herself to pursue any line of thought regarding why wouldn't serve any purpose. Better that they remained far from each other, especially after the embrace he'd given her when they found the braid and photo on the bunk. They'd fit together too well.

She had to stop thinking about him that way. She wouldn't be the second Reilly sister to have her heart broken and her life shattered by this man. Lexie squeezed her eyes shut and pressed the bridge of her nose with her thumb and forefinger.

"Knock, knock?"

Several raps on the door frame followed the question, and three men in navy blue security uniforms entered the room. An older, stocky gentleman who looked as if he'd spent a lifetime on the open water strode over to Shaun and extended his hand. "Tim Parsons. We spoke earlier about the incident on the parking deck?"

"Tim, thank you for bringing your team in here. We've got a bit of an unusual situation." Shaun took the man's hand in a firm grasp, and Lexie noted with mild annoyance that all the security officer offered her was a curt nod.

"Call me Parsons." He jabbed a thumb over his shoulder toward the two men behind him. The shorter of the two had a lanky build with arms that went on for days, and bright orange hair to complement it. He stared at the floor and the walls as though wishing he could be anywhere but inside a passenger's room. The other security officer, however, looked familiar. "Reed and Josh are my main team. We'll do what we can, but as you know, we have our hands full with the recent announcement. What's the situation here?"

Josh seemed to sense her gaze on him and met her look with a nod of acknowledgment. They'd met him in the computer room. Well, a familiar face was a good thing, right?

"Lexie, why don't you have one of the officers escort you to the lounge?" Shaun's question sliced through her brooding thoughts. "I'll meet you there after we get things sorted here."

Escort her to the lounge, as if she was a child? Not likely. "I can see myself there, thank you very much. But this is my room, so I don't see why I should leave."

Parsons cleared his throat, waving his hand in her general direction. "Sorry, miss, but judging by what this gentleman has told me, we'll need to move you to another room while this one is under investigation." He turned back to Shaun. "There's no Royal Canadian Mounted Police on board today, but we'll close off the room until we reach harbor."

Lexie shuffled closer to her bags, away from the door. Being pushed out of whatever was going on wouldn't help her investigation or give her the answers she needed regarding Shaun's latest suggestion. Human trafficking? It sounded absurd, and yet deep in her heart, she knew that some people were fully capable of evil. Was kidnapping people and forcing them into menial labor truly that far-fetched?

"Won't moving me to another room cause the same problem? If somebody got in here, they could get into that room, too. I don't see how that's any safer."

Parsons smiled at her as though she'd lost a few brain cells. "It's a matter of protocol and safety, Miss…"

"Reilly. Lexie Reilly." She didn't bother to cross the room and shake his hand. "Forget about the room. I don't need sleep." She reached down to pick up her bags, but a hand on her arm stopped her mid-motion. She straightened to find Shaun next to her, a sheepish smile on his face.

"It's a good idea, Lexie. Humor me on this and take a different, safer room for the night. The person who accessed your room may have hacked into the passenger list and found your room number there. Your new room won't be on file, so you should be able to get a good night's rest."

Lexie scolded her heart, which threatened to melt at his sincerity. She matched his gaze and held it for a few seconds before realizing that he did, in fact, make a good point about the passenger list. "Fine. But I still want an explanation for how you know all that stuff you told me…understand?"

He nodded and took a step back, easing the growing tension in the air between them. "I'll tell you as much as I can, and that's a promise. But you'll have to meet me halfway. I have some questions for you, too. Meet in the lounge in a half hour or so?"

She agreed, picked up her bags and headed to the door. What could he possibly have to ask her? Compulsion moved her to look back at Shaun one last time before following Reed to her new cabin. He and Parsons were discussing the photo left on her bunk, and despite the lumberjack getup he wore, Shaun's demeanor looked too smooth—too professional for him to simply be a passenger who'd stumbled across her path. And while this thought left her with more suspicions than reassurances, she couldn't help but wonder why she'd felt so much safer in his presence than she had in the few moments she'd been on board alone.

FIVE

After sorting things out with Parsons, Shaun headed back to his room and dug his portable Broadband Global Area Network satellite terminal from his gear bag. He bundled up with a few more layers of warm clothes and jogged to the nearest outer deck exit to set up the phone connection. He was already an hour overdue for his first check-in, which didn't bode well for the upcoming conversation.

"You'd better have something for us, agent," came the gravelly voice of Jack Credicott, the case officer Shaun reported to in Langley, Virginia. "You know how the men upstairs get cranky when we keep them waiting. Either you've caught our man or you're about to bust him. Throw me a nugget, here."

Shaun grinned, imagining Jack at his desk with an oversize mug of Costa Rican coffee and his ubiquitous jar of green Jolly Rancher candies. "I'll do you one better, Jack. I have reason to believe the Wolf has at least one 'package' aboard the ship." He followed the statement by relating the incident on the parking deck and subsequent events. "The cut braid looks like the Wolf's work—just enough violence to make a statement, but not enough to cut into profits."

"So he's either close or you've got yourself into a wasp nest of drones moving packages for him." The crinkle of a plastic wrapper transmitted across the ocean into Shaun's ear.

"I wouldn't say it's a nest. Maybe a barbershop quartet's worth."

"Anyone tell you that you make no sense sometimes, agent?"

"That's four, Jack. Max of four."

The officer chuckled, candy clacking across his teeth. "And the mainland?"

Shaun glanced out at the ocean, but the night had grown too deep to see much of anything. "The Wolf could be waiting at harbor to receive packages, intending to move them elsewhere. Haven't ruled that possibility out yet."

Jack sighed and cleared his throat. "You're close, kid. I don't need to tell you twice to be careful." The weariness in Jack's voice came through loud and clear on Shaun's end. This op had taken a lot out of everyone involved, including the lives of several agents and more than one asset. Not to mention the drain on external relationships—

hence his ongoing singleness since that day eight years ago when he'd told Nicola that they simply weren't right for each other.

With the finish line to the op closer than ever, Shaun needed to ensure that he could protect the people around him without having to lie or coerce them into cooperation. "The woman who was attacked, Alexandra Reilly, could be a valuable asset. She's got her own set of intel on a missing woman she's tracking, which we could use to help triangulate or narrow down the Wolf's position. Plus, she seems to be a direct target at this stage. Keeping her out of harm's way may be to our direct advantage.

"And, uh…" Shaun cleared his throat before continuing. "Point of note? I had a brief friendship and a falling out with her sister. Before the Agency, I mean. It was during the mission trip to Botswana that changed my life. I honestly never thought I'd see either of them again, but the point here is that Lexie Reilly knows my real name. I had to correct her so she wouldn't blow my cover, but this has made her aware I'm using a different name on board. She's not naive, Jack. It's only a matter of time before she starts asking questions."

Jack thought for a moment before responding. "Your call on how deep to involve the asset, then. Might be worth involving ferry security, too." Shaun tried to protest, but Jack cut him off. "Hear me out on this. If you're on a ferry with passengers aboard, and one of them is capable of intense violence to protect his interests, you're going to need help keeping order if things get out of hand. Especially if you're stuck at sea for several days."

Bring the security team into the investigation? Shaun had done similar things before, and in this case it meant having more bodies on the lookout for Lexie and the rest of the passengers. It could be a smart move, depending on how reliable and skilled the ferry security team happened to be. "You sure they won't just get in the way, Jack? Not to question their training for the job, but that's exactly what I'm concerned about. Maybe bring in the captain instead?"

"Bring in security, agent. Use your cover story, and watch your back. There are more people to think about here than just the Wolf. We don't want an international incident on our hands. Emphasize the need for discretion and do what you need to keep them in line, but it sounds like you're going to want all the help you can get. Understood?"

Shaun understood, but that didn't mean he had to like it. Would Lexie be glad to hear he had a legitimate claim to help her, or would she be angry that he'd been less than forthcoming about his role on board thus far? "Hey, Jack? Think you could do a little favor for me?"

The other man's fingers tapped on his keyboard

as Shaun spoke. Jack was likely swamped with work, but Shaun hoped his next request wouldn't be too far out of the realm of possibility.

"Fire away. Not literally, kid." Jack laughed at his own joke. "What is it?"

"Can you search for any intelligence on Alexandra and Nicola Reilly?"

"You want me to do a background on the asset? That's not so unusual. Probably would have done it anyway."

Shaun brushed a lock of stray hair out of his eyes, resting his fingertips on his temple. "I should also mention that the asset is angry at me, and I don't know why."

Jack's tone shifted from handler to amused friend. "Have you tried asking her about it?"

"Not exactly the right timing, as you may have deduced."

"It's never the right timing, agent. As with anything involving assets or outside relationships, you have to make time. I thought you'd have learned that by now."

Shaun's heart tightened. During Shaun's early days at the Agency, the man had coached him through months of personal doubt. Of course his advice was spot on. "It's an easy lesson to remember, but a harder one to practice. I'll try to talk to her, and that's a promise. But can you still look into it for me? I'm not sure when I'll have a chance to call back in, especially if things get dicey. Hold the info until then."

Jack agreed, and Shaun hung up with a heavy weight in his chest. He had to talk to Lexie and tell her the truth—she deserved it, and if he was honest with himself, he cared for her well-being enough to *want* to tell her. More than her well-being, in fact. He cared for *her*, and for a moment in her cabin, it seemed as though she might have begun to care for him, too.

Lexie's new cabin had a similar layout to her old one, with the addition of a coffeemaker and ritzier linens. The location gave the illusion of safety, at least—Josh had pointed out the security office as they passed by, and they'd crossed paths with the captain coming out of his quarters. After dropping her bags off in the room, she intended to head to the lounge, but her stomach rumbled a reminder that she hadn't eaten since lunchtime.

"Can we escort you back to the lounge?" mumbled Reed, the redheaded security officer. He didn't make eye contact as he spoke, as though he also knew how silly the request was as he made it. "Your friend said he'd meet you there."

Lexie shut the cabin door behind her and watched as a couple lumbered through the hallway, suited head-to-toe in heavy winter gear. "The lounge is one floor up and a straight path down the outside deck, right?"

Reed nodded, but his forehead creased with concern. "Sure, but it's mighty cold outside. Wouldn't recommend going outside in this weather. It ain't safe. Slippery out there at night. And your friend made me promise to take you back to the lounge myself."

So, the question had been a formality and she couldn't escape the escort after all. What she wouldn't give for a few minutes to herself to think. She needed time to process everything that had happened, not to mention the oddly heroic actions of Shaun "Lane." If she didn't know any better, she'd peg him for some kind of law enforcement, not a government man.

Her stomach rumbled again, louder this time. Reed glanced sideways at her belly, and heat rose in her cheeks. The events of the past hour had, once again, prevented her from finishing both coffee number two and her bag of trail mix. "I'll be fine," she said, using her go-to dismissal. "I doubt whoever left the message on my bunk is going to try any funny business with so many passengers wandering up and down the halls. From the sound of things, heading to the buffet upstairs is a better option for me."

Despite her insistence that she could make it up two floors to the restaurant on her own, Josh decided that he'd head back to her old quarters to let Shaun know where she'd gone while Reed escorted her to the buffet. They took the elevator up two more floors to the short escalator that took them the rest of the way to the ship's open-concept restaurant. They arrived amidst a massive crowd of passengers, many of whom stood around with worried or anxious expressions on their faces. Lexie suspected that much of the anxiety stemmed from hunger, as hers did, rather than a worry over their delayed arrival in Argentia.

The scent of mashed potatoes, lobster, gravy and fresh biscuits wafted throughout the room, sending Lexie's stomach into a complete tailspin. A giddy little girl passed by holding a plate piled high with battered haddock and French fries smothered in ketchup. Lexie resisted the urge to reach out and snatch a fry off the girl's plate.

"I can take it from here," Lexie said, whirling around to pull her attention from all the loaded plates. "You'll make sure the other guy found Shaun and told him where I went?"

Reed pulled a walkie-talkie from his utility belt and waved it back and forth. "Will do. I gotta get back to help them anyway. You run into any trouble, there are emergency phones around. Pick one up and dial nine, and we'll be on the other end."

Lexie thanked the reserved young officer and watched him walk away. Should she have gone back to get Shaun before heading here? Another glance at the fully laden buffet struck her with a wave of guilt. It wasn't as though Shaun had eaten dinner, either. The temptation to grab a biscuit or a handful of onion rings tugged at her willpower.

She closed her eyes, took a deep breath and turned away from the buffet. It made more sense to wait for Shaun. Plus, now might not be the best time to sit down and spend a half hour eating, not if Maria might actually be aboard the ship. Every second could mean the difference between life and death.

Lexie's stomach roiled at the thought. Fries and gravy didn't seem all that appealing anymore. She slipped down the descending escalator, taking the steps in small hops to make the journey faster. If she moved quickly, perhaps she could catch Shaun on his way here, and redirect the both of them to the lounge for a coffee and granola bar.

She recalled Shaun's cryptic statements in her room after they'd found the braid and photograph. He'd known far too much about human trafficking to simply be a casual passenger on this ship. Pulse pounding in her ears, Lexie stopped when she came to a branching hallway. She hadn't been paying attention to where she was going, too lost in urgent thoughts. She turned right and found herself in a short corridor with a metal crash-bar door at the end. A bright-red exit sign hung at the top. The door looked similar to the one by the stairs that led up from the parking deck, so she pushed on the door, intending to walk down the two flights of stairs instead of continuing to search for the elevator.

Lexie jumped back with a yelp as a blast of freezing cold air slammed into her face. The heavy door fell back into place as she backed out of the little corridor. What had Reed said? Taking the outer deck could be dangerous at night. Too slippery. Fine, she'd find another way.

Her attempt to retrace her steps proved more difficult than expected, and it took only a few minutes to realize she'd wandered even farther off course than before. All the passenger doors looked the same, closed and silent, with only the hum of the ship's inner workings to let her know there was still life aboard. *Where is everyone? A staff member would be really handy right about now...*

"Miss? Are you lost?"

Lexie jumped, alarmed that someone could sneak up on her in this quiet area of the ship. Her shoulders loosened, seeing a familiar face. "Security officer Josh, thank goodness."

Josh brightened as he recognized her. "Miss Reilly! I thought you were headed up to find dinner?"

"I thought I'd wait for Shaun," she admitted, feeling sheepish at being caught wandering the halls. "I wanted to head back to my old cabin and see if he was still there, but I started thinking about everything that had happened and took a few wrong turns."

Josh pointed a thumb over his shoulder. "Elevator's back that way, stairs are past them at the far end. Can I walk you down there? Shaun actually sent me back to find you. He said he'd be a few minutes longer."

"I guess so. I honestly don't know where I am. Lead the way."

When they reached the elevator, Josh punched the button for two floors down. The elevator rose through the shaft with a high-pitched screech. "Uh, forget you heard that. I promise it's safe. I was actually on my way to see the maintenance team about it. If you can believe it, the maintenance elevators a few doors down are even worse."

"That's mildly reassuring. I've had enough excitement for one day." They rode the elevator to the correct floor, Lexie only breaking the silence when the doors opened with a quiet ding. "Thanks. Which direction?"

Josh pointed to the right. "Head that way for Shaun. Two left turns and you'll be in the correct hall."

Lexie thanked him and trudged down the hall, turning left at the end. However, the hall she ended up in had several branching hallways, each looking similar to the other. Was she supposed to take the first left, or just find the hall with the right room numbers?

As she stood contemplating which hall to take, she felt a prickle on the back of her neck. She whirled around, fully expecting to see someone behind her, but the hall was empty. She needed to make a decision.

Lexie took the first hall to her left, but only managed a few steps before freezing in place. It truly felt as if she was being watched, but when she turned to look, she was confronted once again by an empty hall.

After the third time, she couldn't take it anymore. Whether someone was following her or not, she wasn't going to play the sitting duck and give them an open target. With a sudden burst of speed, Lexie turned down the closest hallway and bolted.

SIX

Shaun exited his room deep in thought, contemplating the least contentious way to let Lexie know about the op without compromising his cover. Straight-to-the-point honesty seemed like the best choice, as usual. She was smart and would be able to fill in any obvious blanks.

He pulled his door shut just as Lexie careened around a corner and barreled straight into him. Shaun's feet flew out from under him and they tumbled to the floor in a tangle of limbs. "Hello to you, too," he wheezed, enjoying the deepening pink on Lexie's cheeks perhaps more than he should.

"Sorry," she stammered, her apology coming out thin and breathless. "I thought someone was following me, and then a headache came on without warning…"

Shaun rose to his feet and offered his hand. To his surprise, she forewent the look of disdain and instead grasped his outstretched palm. Her hand felt soft and warm, and he regretted having to let go. "Are you feeling all right now?"

"Aside from a bruised ego? More or less. The headache is subsiding, believe it or not." She brushed a tumble of hair out of her eyes and reached behind her head to straighten her hair clip. "Sorry, again."

"Don't worry about it. I was lost in thought myself, coming out the door. But now that you're here—"

"We need to talk," they said in unison.

A hint of amusement appeared at the corner of Lexie's lips. "I could use another coffee," she said. "And a snack. Are you hungry? The buffet is busy but open. It smells amazing."

Shaun had to admit that he'd been starving for the past hour, but a crowded, noisy room didn't sound like the best place for a serious conversation. He suggested the lounge instead, which turned out to be the right call. Only a few couples and a solo traveler remained in the area, sipping paper cups of tea and coffee.

Shaun chose a table in the opposite corner. He made a quick call through to Parsons on one of the wall-mounted emergency phones before ordering two coffees from the coffee bar.

"One cream," he said, setting the cup down in front of Lexie. Her eyes widened in surprise, then softened as he took his seat.

"You remembered," she murmured, taking off the lid to cool the hot beverage faster. "Impressive."

"I aim to please," he replied, realizing how cliché it sounded the moment the words left his mouth. Still, it brought a figment of a smile to her lips, so he shoved aside the regret. What would it take to make her smile without reservation? "But before I get to my news," he said, feeling bold, "we need to clear up a few things. Have I done something to offend you?"

Lexie's gaze dropped as she blew on the surface of her coffee. "I don't see how that's relevant to the immediate situation." Her jawline hardened and a heavy silence descended on their table.

Shaun swallowed hard on his next sip of coffee, the liquid scalding the back of his throat as it slid down. "I'll take that as a yes. What did I do?"

Lexie scowled and folded her arms across her chest, leaning back in her chair. "You know exactly what you did. Or have you broken so many hearts since Nikki that you can't even remember back that far?"

Her words felt like a jolt of electricity in the brain. "Broken hearts? What are you talking about? We were just friends. I mean, near the end of the trip she told me she wanted more, but I explained I wasn't interested in a relationship and we left it at that."

Lexie shook her head, refusing to make eye contact. "And now you're a liar, too. I thought you'd become a nicer person, based on the past few hours, but I guess I was wrong."

It was like a giant vacuum had sucked all the air from the room. Lexie's sister had lied to her? Why? To what end? "I promise you, I wasn't aware of any broken hearts. The mission trip changed me, Lexie. All that poverty and suffering...I knew it was time to put away the past and get serious."

That got her attention. She stared at him, incredulous. "I don't believe you. Nikki and I were close. I saw how hurt she was by you, let her cry on my shoulder and dealt with the fallout when we got home. I watched her fall to pieces, Shaun."

Shaun tried to process what she'd said. "Were close? Not anymore?"

"Yes, *were*. Obviously that's not the case now."

"I'm afraid I don't understand. Did she move away?"

Lexie's expression remained flat and uninviting. "You know very well what happened." Her scowl faltered as Shaun felt his jaw drop. "She told me that she thought you two were a couple, that you kissed her and led her on before dumping her for another girl. I told her to forget you, that you didn't know what you were missing..." Her voice lowered to a whisper, and she stared at her hands on the table.

"Lexie." Shaun reached across and covered her hands with his own. Clearly her sister had kept the truth from her for some reason. "We were just friends. Nothing happened between us that summer. Nikki was fun to be around and we had a lot of laughs, but I wasn't interested in her that way. A relationship was the furthest thing from my mind, and I was honest with her when she told me she wanted more than friendship."

Lexie sighed, but didn't pull her hands away. "She told me you were cruel, that you'd used her for a disposable summer fling. She used that as an excuse to date a real jerk of a guy when we got back from the trip. I thought it was part of her getting over her heartbreak. Now you're telling me it was just immaturity?"

Shaun swallowed the growing lump in his throat. "Sounds like we've both been taken for a ride."

Lexie finally looked up, meeting his eyes with a sadness that tugged at his heart. He wanted to reach across the table and brush away the tear forming in the corner of her eye before it escaped, but resisted the urge. "She was a complete mess, Shaun, so I'm having a lot of trouble believing what you're saying is true."

"I promise I'm telling the truth."

Lexie frowned. "She was used to guys falling all over her and I think she knew her rebound guy was a terrible influence, but she claimed he gave her the attention she deserved... Now that I say it out loud, it sounds like a terrible excuse. And now I can't even ask her about it. I don't know what to believe."

"Can't ask her about it? Why not?" Shaun still reeled from Lexie's revelation. What more could there possibly be to say about this situation? "We both deserved our wild-child status for a while there, but I can't imagine..."

"She's gone, Shaun."

How many more surprises could he take?

"She disappeared a few months after the trip. Vanished with barely a trace, all evidence suggesting she ran off with this guy."

Shaun sensed there was more to her statement than she'd said. Lexie bit her bottom lip and eyed him from beneath her lashes. Lexie, who worked to find missing people. Who panicked about not messing up this job. Who refused to give up on those law enforcement had given up on.

Suddenly, it all made sense. "You think she may have been kidnapped?"

Lexie's nod was nearly imperceptible, her voice even quieter. "I keep working on these cases, searching for girls like Maria."

Shaun heard the unspoken words. She hoped for clues, indications, anything that might point to Nikki's whereabouts. Nikki, the wild, beautiful girl he'd thought he had let down gently, but who'd instead used his rejection as an excuse to spiral her life out of control when she didn't get what she wanted…who'd lied to her kind, compassionate sister. No wonder Lexie had been angry at seeing him again.

Shaun never would have fallen for someone like Lexie in the past. She'd been too Goody-Two-Shoes, too "safe" for him back then, but people changed. Priorities changed. *He'd* changed. That's why he'd said no to Nikki after the mission trip.

He couldn't begin to imagine how Lexie must be feeling, realizing she'd believed her sister's lie for so many years. Could he really blame Lexie for acting so hostile toward him? What could he do to prove the truth of what happened in the past?

"Do you think—" he began, but his words were cut short by the arrival of Head of Security Parsons and security team member Josh. Parsons was growling into his walkie-talkie, but offered a terse nod of acknowledgment to Shaun.

"What do you mean, you don't know if it's important? Of course it's important," Parsons snapped. "Get back down there and find him! Ridiculous." He shoved the walkie-talkie back onto his belt.

"Good evening, gentlemen," Shaun said, hoping to diffuse the tension.

"This had better be important," drawled Parsons. "We're swamped here. People are panicking about being stuck at sea, even though we have enough food to feed them for a week. You'd think they have no idea how a modern watercraft operates. And I just got a call from my young guy, the redheaded kid. He came across some joker trying to sneak into a restricted area, or should I say, he passed the guy in the hallway and then called to ask if that might be a concern. Can you believe it? Reed's a good kid but he's short a few marbles, if you get my meaning."

"Interesting." Shaun felt his hopes rising, despite knowing it could be nothing at all. "How'd the passenger manage that?"

"Maintenance elevator," Josh said, nodding to Lexie, who remained seated at the table. "Told you we needed to get those fixed."

"Does he have the man in custody? Someplace I can talk to him?"

"Whoa, whoa." Parsons held his palms aloft. "Slow down. Want to give me a reason why I should let you do that?"

Shaun glanced around the room to ensure that no other ears were within hearing distance. He needed to be careful about how much he told anyone, but as Jack had said, moving around covertly on a passenger ferry would require the cooperation of the security team. And if they'd caught a passenger snooping around, Shaun absolutely wanted to question the guy.

"I'm only going to say this once. Time is a factor here." He checked to make sure Lexie could hear him. She stood and rounded the table to stand next to him, coffee in hand. "How much do you guys know about human trafficking?"

Parsons huffed, crossing his arms. "I've heard of smuggling drugs and guns, but people? Sounds a little extreme."

Shaun figured as much. He was no stranger to hearing denial on the subject. "Lexie and I chatted about this earlier, but it's a real problem happening under the noses of North American citizens. One ring in particular abducts young women here and abroad, with the ringleader—known only as the Wolf—working with a pack of accomplices. He preys on those he perceives as weak, encircling and snaring them with lies of a better life."

"Don't know what this has to do with us," Parsons said. "Or you, for that matter."

Shaun cleared his throat, shot a glance at Lexie and hoped she'd forgive him for this later. "Miss Reilly is searching for one of these young women, and I'm helping her do so." He heard Lexie's sharp intake of breath, but avoided meeting her eyes. He'd explain later, insomuch as he could. "I believe the woman she's searching for has fallen victim to one of the Wolf's schemes, and it has also put Miss Reilly in the line of fire. The events of the day match up to the Wolf's modus operandi." *Take him out, the whole ring collapses,* Shaun added to himself. "Miss Reilly boarded the ferry intending to find and remove one of his revenue sources. Each girl is worth a lot of money to a trafficker, and by searching for Maria, she's threatening not only his income, but his entire operation as a whole."

Shaun watched a struggle play out on Lexie's face as she tried to fight past the urge of denial—and the urge to punch him in the nose, most likely. He didn't blame her, but the search for Maria provided the perfect cover for his own search or the Wolf.

"You suspect someone on board is this Wolf? A passenger?" Lexie eyed him with a *you owe me* look. "It could be anyone."

"It could." Shaun hated turning Lexie's suspicions up a notch, but if it kept her alive, it'd be worth it. He'd seen firsthand what traffickers would do to protect their interests, and it wasn't pretty. "We know he's male, but because of the pack mentality of the operation, that's literally all the physical description we have to go on. The passenger you caught sneaking around would be a good place to start, though."

Parsons tilted his chin upward, frowning. "Look, kid. I've been in the ferry security business for years, and I've never heard of such a thing. Drugs, yes. Cops caught one of those rings a few years back, but people? That's harder to do, isn't it? We'd notice. Plus, do you really think Newfoundland is where they'd take her? Why not the Pacific? Taking people across the Atlantic sounds backward."

"That's a question I plan to get an answer to, the moment I have this man in custody. Remember, these people are professionals. And dangerous. I'd prefer if you and your team handled damage control in the meantime. I'll get my hands dirty and radio you in for help when we need it, but your primary concern needs to remain on the passengers of this vessel. If they get wind of this, we'll have mass panic on our hands, and since we're stuck at sea..."

"It ain't gonna be pretty. I get it. But you still haven't told me why I should trust you instead of waiting for the Coast Guard."

"I work for the United States government," Shaun admitted. "As I said, I'm searching for this girl, too. And look at it this way—you've got a ferry full of passengers to take care of and a possible international incident on your hands if the Wolf or one of his lackeys is on board. You're going to need all the help you can get. Lexie and I will do the heavy lifting while you manage crowd control."

With a sigh of resignation, Parsons pulled his walkie-talkie from his belt and fiddled with the dials. "Government, eh? Fine. Take this one, I'll grab another from my office. Call when you need us."

Accumulated tension eased from Shaun's shoulders. The authoritative routine didn't always work, but this security team was already in over their heads. A person exuding confidence tended to be a welcome presence in dire situations.

"One more thing," Shaun said as the men turned to leave. "Don't tell anyone else what's going on. The safety of the passengers and this girl may be at stake. The last thing we need is someone running scared, making rash moves or disappearing as soon as we hit the dock. Any news on the passenger, Parsons?"

"Right." Parsons radioed through to Reed, who didn't pick up. "He's probably held up someplace. I'll track him down and fill you in." The security personnel began walking away, but Parsons turned around and paused. "You know, if everything's as you say, I don't think the kidnapper running scared is what we'll need to worry about."

Glancing at Lexie, Shaun couldn't agree with him more. *That's what I'm afraid of.*

On the inside, Lexie reeled from the conversation of the past five minutes. Had Nikki actually lied to her eight years ago? Was her sister the one who'd gone after Shaun, and not vice-versa? All this time, Lexie had carried around disgust and anger at the boy who'd stolen her sister's heart on a mission trip only to stomp on it without warning... except it hadn't been that way at all. Or had it?

Lexie pressed the base of her palm against her forehead to ease the growing pressure. Who did she believe? Reconciling this strong, compassionate man across from her with her sister's story would be impossible had she not seen this version of Shaun in action.

Perhaps proving even more difficult to believe was what he'd just told the security officers. Combined with giving a different last name to the medical staff—she *knew* she hadn't remembered that wrong—something else was going on here. Something she doubted Shaun would willingly tell her on his own, so she decided to take a direct approach.

"Changed your last name when you started working for the government, did you?"

He flinched at her accusation, and Lexie pressed her lips together to suppress a knowing smile. After a few beats of silence, Shaun ran his fingers through his hair, offering up a disarming grin.

"It's like I said, I work for the US government."

Lexie said nothing and stared him down, waiting. Shaun chuckled, looked around to double check that they were alone in the room, and leaned in closer to Lexie. "You're very perceptive, Reilly. Yes, I did have to change my name. I'm CIA and I need to protect my cover. As you can tell, I didn't count on bumping into someone from my past. It happens less often than you'd think."

Lexie stifled a gasp as a thrill crept up her spine, which she immediately tamped down on. Shaun Carver, CIA? And yet, she believed him. His coffee-brown eyes pleaded with her for trust and understanding, and for a moment, she was tempted to give it to him.

To distract herself—and to possibly drown the migrating stomach butterflies—she drained the remainder of her coffee, grateful to have at least some sustenance in her stomach. "You've been doing this awhile, I take it?"

A flicker of annoyance crossed Shaun's features. Did he think she'd just drop it? The man had willingly put himself in possible danger on two occasions already, and despite herself, Lexie felt her heart warming at the depth of Shaun's concern for both her and others. It was an undeniable and unavoidable change from the version of him she'd thought to be true, almost magnetic, compelling her to want to know more about him. To get a little closer. And yet, that would compromise her focus. Besides, they both had a serious job to do.

"Let's just say I've spent the past three years on

the trail of some very dangerous people." Shaun pushed away from the chair he leaned on. "We should get back to the search, if you're ready. Try to piece the clues together."

He had a point. They did no good by sitting around. "Fine. But if what you've told us puts Maria in danger—"

Shaun rubbed a hand down his face. "Honestly, right now? It's not only Maria I'm worried about. Anything we tackle from this point onward, we tackle together. You've already been targeted, and I don't trust the Wolf to leave you alone until he's convinced you've given up on the girl."

"Which I haven't. And I won't."

"Trust me, I understand. I'm not going to try and talk you out of it."

"You won't? Won't I compromise your operation or whatever?"

Shaun's gentle laugh sent a rush of warmth to her center. It was a reassuring sound in a tense moment, but she clamped down on the urge to fully let her guard down, regardless of his undeniable sincerity. She still hadn't decided if she believed him.

"You've just become part of the operation," Shaun said, interrupting her thoughts. "But let's keep that between us, shall we?" His seriousness with those final words only vanished once she'd nodded agreement. He then motioned for her to follow him, and they exited the lounge in silence.

Shaun positioned himself about two feet behind her as they checked the public rooms on the deck, searching for any sign of disturbance or possible person-sized hiding spaces.

Even at this distance, Lexie found herself fully aware of Shaun's presence. He matched her every step and every turn, ensuring he'd be within arm's reach should they come across any danger. In a way, it was comforting, but having him so close brought up unwelcome feelings that were getting harder to bury.

As they exited a small cloak room, Lexie couldn't help but notice Shaun's build as he glanced from one side to another down the hallway. With such broad shoulders and chest, anyone who didn't know what he did might mistake him for a construction worker or logger. Of course, his plaid shirt and puffy vest didn't help. She supposed not all spies wore suits and dark sunglasses, despite what she'd seen on television.

"Library," Shaun said behind her. Lexie stopped and touched the door on their right. "Even if there's nothing in there, we might as well sit down and go over what we have so far."

"You mean, the nothing we have so far?" Lexie entered the room and Shaun closed the library door behind them. Six-foot-high shelves lined the walls of the small room, and several armchairs and coffee tables were strategically placed in small groups or singles. Lexie's shoulders dropped by an inch as her tension began to melt away. Shelves of books tended to have that effect, enveloping her with a sense of peace. Shaun surveyed the room with an impassive gaze, tucking his hands in his back pockets.

"This is nice," he said. Lexie gaped at him, barely believing her ears. He caught her eye and shrugged. "No, really. I don't get to read much, but if I wanted to get away from the bustle of a busy ferry trip, I'd come here. Something tells me you would, too." He watched her curiously, as though seeing her through a magnifying lens.

Lexie rolled her shoulders back, trying to ease the discomfort of feeling examined. "Yes, I would. Deductive reasoning from a trained agent?"

"Or a good memory from the distant past?" He winced and looked back toward the door. "But you might want to be careful how loud you throw the *A* word around. It's not a feature we want to advertise. Right now I think we have the element of surprise, with the Wolf knowing only of your purpose here, not mine, as far as we know. This should give us an advantage both in keeping you safe and in searching for Maria, though that could change at any moment."

Shaun walked around the room's perimeter,

checking behind tables and tapping on the sides of shelves. Lexie followed suit, starting at the other end of the room until they met in the middle. The final shelf yielded no secrets, which didn't surprise Lexie. Searching rooms had seemed like a good idea until they'd come up empty in one place after another. She still wasn't entirely sure what they were searching for, but Shaun had ideas about intelligence gathering from subtle clues that she couldn't very well argue with.

She leaned against the final shelf as Shaun swept his hand across the top, coming away with a handful of gray dust for his efforts.

He raised his eyebrows and held his palm up toward her. "Huh. Dust at sea. I had no idea."

Lexie suppressed a laugh. The man had saved her from being choked to death and hadn't hesitated to enter her room when he thought someone dangerous might be inside, but a sprinkling of dust stopped him in his tracks. "Where there are people, there's dust, Mr. Lane. Or did you think the sea automatically vacuumed it out of the air?"

"Guess I never thought about it," he said, wiping the dust on his jeans. "Dusting at sea just seems… wrong, somehow."

Lexie couldn't hold back the laugh this time, but as her giggle escaped, she became acutely aware of just how close Shaun stood to her. Her breath caught as he smiled at her, and in the strangeness of the moment, she found herself unable to move away.

"There doesn't seem to be anything here," she said, her voice barely above a whisper. "We haven't found what we're looking for."

He swallowed hard, and Lexie thought she saw a bead of sweat break out on his forehead, despite the cool air of the ship.

"I wouldn't say that," he said, his voice deep and smooth.

The kindness and determination in Shaun's eyes sent a shiver through Lexie from head to toe, the space beyond Shaun becoming hazy and dim. Her lips parted without warning, though she willed them to close. This couldn't be happening. She couldn't be here in this room with him, alone. Too much was at stake, and she risked too much by letting him come this close. Knowing what she did now about Maria's possible circumstances, neither of them could afford this kind of distraction.

Her voice cracked as she forced out the words she hoped would trip the breaker of the static building between them. "Shaun, I can't believe you—"

A click at the door shattered the moment, snapping Lexie back to full awareness of her surroundings. She launched herself away from Shaun's side and reached the library door in four strides.

Lexie gripped the door handle and turned, but

it didn't budge. Adrenaline rushed her senses and a wave of internal heat threatened to drag her into the terrifying oblivion of a panic attack. "We're locked in," she said, pounding a fist on the door. How could she have allowed herself to be so distracted? And by Shaun Carver, of all people—

"Lexie, stop!" Shaun reached her side and tore her fist away from the door, covering her knuckles with his hand. "There's no need to assume the worst. Maybe someone locked it with us inside by accident, shutting areas down for the night. They could have heard your banging and be out there right now, trying to find the right key."

"Or I could have got the attention of the wrong person," she moaned. "What am I thinking?" Lexie yanked her fist away from Shaun and stalked to the other side of the room, feeling the need to get as far away from him as possible. "Call security on your walkie-talkie. Have them come let us out."

Shaun pulled the walkie-talkie out of his belt and turned the top dials, fiddling with them to clear up the static. He grunted, smacking the unit against his hand. "I thought Parsons put this on the right channel, but I must have bumped it. Hang tight."

Lexie pressed her index fingers into the corners of her eyes, hoping to stave off the growing pressure in her skull. She wrinkled her nose at a sudden unpleasant smell and sniffed the air as a second hissing noise joined the walkie-talkie's static. "Do you hear that?"

She visually scanned the room, looking for an escape as the smell of rotten eggs grew stronger. "You smell that?" she asked, feeling oddly light-headed. "What is that?"

Shaun swayed on his feet, coughed and sniffed the air. He regarded her with grave seriousness, a complete one-eighty from their interaction moments before. "That's hydrogen sulfide gas. And it will kill us in minutes if we don't find a way out."

SEVEN

Shaun looked around the room, searching for the gas's entry point. He saw it at the same moment Lexie did—a clear hose, inserted underneath the library door. Taking a deep breath, Shaun dropped to the floor and scooted to the door's edge, trying to see underneath. An opaque film obscured any sight of the hallway, and the crack was too small to fit his fingers through.

"The bottom of the door is taped over," he said, standing. "Look for something that we can put against the hose."

Lexie grabbed cushions off the plush chairs and tossed them to him. "Will those work?"

Shaun began stacking the cushions on and around the hose. "It won't stop the gas from coming inside, but maybe we can slow its progress enough to find a way out of here."

"What about tying fabric around our mouths? It smells terrible." Lexie held a hand over her face, using her other hand to pound on the door at random intervals. "I feel dizzy."

Shaun yanked the walkie-talkie from his belt again and continued turning the dials, trying to find the right channel for the security team. If they didn't get a hold of someone in the next minute, they were in serious trouble. They were both having trouble remaining upright, which meant it wouldn't be long now before their respiratory systems gave out. Just five minutes of exposure to hydrogen sulfide could be lethal. "Find the room's emergency phone."

"It's not working," Lexie cried, seconds later. She stumbled across the room toward him, banging into furniture.

Shaun coughed, feeling tightness in his lungs with each breath. For once, he had no idea what to do. "Sit down, try not to exert yourself. Here, take the radio—turn the top dials until you hear someone. I'll keep looking for something to break the door down."

She nodded sleepily, but took the device from his hands. By sheer willpower, Shaun dragged a nearby coffee table toward the door, forcing his feet to take each step. Maybe he could dislodge the door handle and release whatever had locked it in place from the outside. Maybe he could punch his way through the door. Maybe he could...

His thoughts became jumbled and scattered as he heard Lexie shout into the walkie-talkie.

"Hello? Anyone, please...library...locked in..." Lexie coughed and the walkie-talkie tumbled to the floor. Static crackled from the speaker, and Lexie's prone form stretched out on the chair, motionless.

He'd failed. He'd promised to keep her safe, and he'd failed. Why would anyone do this to them? Did the Wolf want Lexie out of the way that badly? The irony of the situation didn't fail to escape him—Lexie had acted incredulous that someone could be trying to kill her, and yet here was undeniable proof. But she'd never get the chance to acknowledge his need to keep her safe, because it would be only a matter of seconds before both of them succumbed to the gas pumping into the room. Permanently.

Shaun's legs gave out, and his knees cracked against the library floor. He placed his hands on his lap to stop from falling all the way over. Lexie hadn't moved for the past fifteen seconds, and Shaun's heart ached. Why hadn't he told her how deep his affection had grown in just a few short hours? Why had they met again after nearly a decade, only to lose each other to the cruelty of an unknown villain? *I trust You, Lord, but I don't understand.*

He crawled across the floor with shaking limbs

and rattling breath, reaching for Lexie's hand. It felt cold and clammy. The walkie-talkie still crackled, and his vision had become a complete blur of muted shades. He'd failed, and this was the end.

Something banged on the door as Shaun's world turned black.

"Come on, Lexie. Wake up." Shaun held the petite brunette's hand between his palms, rubbing warmth back into them. She'd been out for too long, the oxygen mask covering her soft, pink lips for the past forty-five minutes since he'd regained consciousness. The onboard nurse had chalked her delayed recovery up to their size difference, though the nurse's initial assessment stated that they hadn't inhaled a strong enough dosage of hydrogen sulfide to do lasting damage. They'd need to take care for the next seventy-two hours, as symptoms of lung damage could show up at any point during that period, but they'd been rescued literally in the nick of time.

If Parsons hadn't barged through the door when he did, they could have been facing permanent eye damage, respiratory failure, cardiac arrest or complete cardiac failure. That the culprit who'd set up the gas trap had wanted them dead, Shaun had no doubt. It was only by chance—and God's grace—that their exposure had been midlevel and short-term.

"Let her rest," Parsons said, sauntering to Shaun's side. Shaun glanced past Parsons to see the two ubiquitous members of Parsons's security crew standing watch at the door. It was a thoughtful but unnecessary gesture. They had plenty of other passengers to deal with.

Shaun shook his head and squeezed Lexie's hand. "You know I can't do that, not when there's someone aboard trying to kill her. The nurse says she'll wake up soon."

Parsons nodded and gestured to his men. "If you want to head out and get something to eat, or bring back a tea for her when she wakes up or whatever, we can keep an eye out here. My boys know not to let anyone else in aside from medical."

"No, thanks. I can't risk that whoever gassed us could cause a distraction elsewhere on the ship and force you guys to leave her here unprotected. I don't mind waiting around. She'll want answers when she wakes up."

"You think it's likely someone might try more funny business this soon?" Parsons crossed his arms, taking a wide stance. "Gotta say, I don't like this happening on my ship. Makes me look like I can't do my job."

Shaun empathized with the man. Getting bested by an unknown culprit on one's own turf tended to be more than a little disheartening. It wouldn't surprise Shaun if the burly man had begun questioning his ability to run the ship's security at all.

"Don't be too hard on yourself," Shaun said, cuffing the man on the arm. "Whoever is after Lexie saw an opportunity and took it. I suspect they saw us searching the decks and took advantage of the moment." He'd already gone back to check the room out with one of the medical staff. Everything—tape, hose, tubing—had been removed, and no one had owned up to it. "The equipment and chemicals needed for hydrogen gas aren't hard to come by. Most supply closets have everything a person needs for it. You guys have a policy to lock up supply areas?"

Parsons grunted and trained his gaze on the floor. "Between you and me? Yeah, on most levels. The boys in engineering and maintenance get a little sloppy though, since there's no passenger admittance down there. So long as they do their job right and no one gets hurt, I don't police the little things. That's up to management."

Shaun had been afraid of that. "And the passenger Reed ran into?"

"Engine level. Hey, Reed?"

Reed poked his head around the door. "Boss?"

"You find that nosy passenger yet?"

"No, boss."

Parsons rolled his eyes and addressed Shaun. "I'll go deal with that. We'll find him, but you let me know if there's anything else the boys and I can do, all right?"

"Sure thing. Quick question, though." Shaun considered how to ask his question without raising the man's ire. "Reed and Josh, they've been with you a long while?"

Parsons frowned, his eyebrows scrunching together in suspicion. "I've been in this business nigh on twenty years, kid. You think I wouldn't know a bad apple if I saw one?"

Shaun shrugged. "Two years? Six months?"

"Josh came on eleven months ago. Reed's a year and a half in."

"You know them well?"

"Well enough." Parsons jabbed a finger in the air at Shaun. "And I don't appreciate what you're implying, government man. Remember, I'm only letting you in on this because you asked nicely."

Not quite the truth, but Shaun would let him win this one. He kept silent as the man stepped from the room, summoning his team to follow.

The moment Parsons left the room, Lexie's fingers curled in Shaun's palm.

His heart fluttered. He couldn't believe it—how could this woman have such an effect on him? That moment in the library, she'd been so close to him. From the top of his head to the tips of his toes, he'd fought to resist the urge to turn the moment into something else. There'd been enough electricity in the air between them to power a lightbulb. Maybe three.

And yet, she'd been all too ready to pull away from him when danger arrived. After all that had happened since they met on the parking deck, could he blame her?

Lexie's eyelids flickered like tiny butterfly wings and pulled open. She blinked several times as her eyes adjusted to the light before focusing on Shaun. He called the nurse over, who removed the oxygen mask, checked her vitals and warned her to stay put and rest for a bit longer.

With the nurse out of sight, Lexie pounced. "What happened? How did we get out?"

Joy welled up in Shaun's chest at the sound of her feisty, if imperious, voice. Of course she'd want to get right down to business. "One thing at a time. We were rescued, believe it or not."

Her eyebrows pulled together in confusion. "How? We didn't get through on the walkie-talkie."

He shrugged. He'd been in just as much disbelief, but being saved from a fatal gassing at the final moment wasn't the first close call he'd had in the field. "God is good, I guess. Plus, Parsons said he heard you through the static. We must have been one notch off on the dial."

Lexie squeezed her eyes shut, yawned and

blinked them open again. "I assume we don't know who did it."

"No one was caught, and there's no fingerprinting kit on board to try and match prints with passengers. We do know the gas was homemade. Hydrogen sulfide requires materials that aren't hard to find on board."

"On board? Isn't that dangerous? Why would the ferry have those ingredients?"

Shaun wished he could tell her it had been a fluke, but the reality was, homemade gasses and bombs were all too easy to throw together in a pinch with standard household items. He'd been up against both more than once.

She closed her eyes again when he explained how the hydrogen gas had been made and delivered. "So we're dealing with someone who knows the ferry, or has a passing familiarity with these ships. They know where to find things," she said, eyes still closed.

Shaun blinked in surprise at her deduction. The woman in front of him was not only brave, but incredibly smart as well. "Exactly. It could be a frequent passenger, someone who uses this kind of vessel to move people along the route regularly. If he's well-recognized and liked by the crew, he could finagle his way into restricted areas of the ship reserved for staff. Or sneak into an area where the storage closets aren't always locked."

"What about the passenger list? The captain or the security team should have a copy. Maybe we could call into Atlantic Voyages's main office to get information on the passengers. If the wireless is working, they could email it through."

What Shaun wouldn't give to be able to kiss her right now. *Settle down, buddy,* he scolded himself. "That's the best idea I've heard all day. I'll call down to Parsons and have him bring us a copy."

"Perfect," Lexie said, shifting on the medical gurney. She propped herself up on her elbows. "Want me to go down to the computer room and make sure we can get online?"

"Whoa! Slow down, soldier." As much as Shaun appreciated her enthusiasm, they'd both been through a lot. "Another attempt was made on your life less than two hours ago. You might want to sit this one out. If you'd like, I can see if the captain will let you rest in the captain's quarters? It has high security, and isn't easily accessed by anyone aside from the captain and the security team. I'd rather not take you back to your room just yet— whoever gassed the library could conceivably trap you in there and finish the job."

He hated to state it in such a blatant way, but sugarcoating the danger wouldn't help either of them.

"No, thanks." Lexie swung her legs over the side of the gurney and hopped to the floor, stumbling slightly as she landed. Shaun winced and reached out to steady her, remembering his own wobbly attempt to stand up a little while ago.

"You're in danger, Lexie. Serious danger."

Lexie stared at him, fire in her eyes. "So is Maria. I have to find her, Shaun."

Shaun shook his head. "It's not worth it. Rest here and let me do my job, and then we can—"

She cut him off with a wave. "You don't understand. I *have* to find her. This is not optional. I'm doing this, and I won't let this Wolf character scare me off. Her family needs her, and her future…she wants to be a veterinarian. Vet school, Shaun. Maria failed algebra three times, got a tutor and went to summer school to pass the class so she can apply for a veterinary program this fall. Are you telling me that I should sit back and leave her survival up to a bunch of strangers when I have the means to do something about it?"

Her comment stung. "I'm not a stranger, Lexie."

"Aren't you?"

The silence that followed her outburst filled the room, catching in the cracks and corners until Shaun couldn't take it anymore.

"Fine," he said, resting his hand lightly on her cheek. "But we're doing this together."

EIGHT

"We'll have to search all the storage areas for any missing toilet bowl cleaner, insecticide or bath products containing sulfur," Shaun said into the phone receiver. Lexie could barely make sense of his words through the buzzing in her ears, but she willed herself to focus. She swallowed hard at the memory of their closeness in the library. She should never have allowed him that close—she should have run at the first sign of weakness. But he'd touched her hand with such tenderness as she'd woken up…and while she'd never in a million years have dreamed that she could feel any kind of affection toward Shaun, she'd be lying to herself if she said she regretted having recrossed paths.

Still, she needed to avoid any future library-like incidents, despite these ridiculous feelings. What would happen if he ever did kiss her? Not that she wanted him to, of course. Why give him the chance to break a second Reilly's heart? She scrunched her eyes shut, unable to escape that destructive train of thought. It only proved how wrong he was for her.

She sucked as much air into her still-burning lungs as possible, centering her attention on Shaun's words. "Lexie and I will take the lower decks and you guys stay up here near the passengers. It's going to be awfully suspicious if a passenger sees us pawing through broom closets, so better that we stay in the areas with less foot traffic."

Shaun hung up and returned to her gurney, hopping up to sit with his legs dangling over the edge. "The nurse asked you to lie down while I was on the phone. It wouldn't hurt to take her advice."

Lexie leaned against the makeshift bed, glad for the rest, but frustrated by the feeling of weakness. "What's a little gassing now and again? I'll be fine. What'd you and the guys decide?"

He didn't take her diversion bait. "It's all right to admit you need a break once in a while, Lexie. That's not weakness. Admitting the need to slow down takes more strength than it does to keep going, at times. I speak from experience."

In her heart, she knew he made a good point, but in her head? Slowing meant time lost, and time lost meant more opportunity for someone to get hurt. "I'm coming with you on your search, Shaun. I can rest when we've got everything figured out."

A knock outside the door diverted their attention, and Parsons strode in with a key dangling between his fingers. "Here you are, kids. This should get you into most locked places. Storage rooms are clearly marked, but there are a few maps of ship schematics near the lower stairwells. We put 'em up as part of evacuation prep protocol a few years ago. Guess they'll finally come in handy."

"Great. Stay in contact." Shaun took the key and slipped it into his pocket, patting the walkie-talkie on his belt with an index finger. "You adjusted this, right?"

Parsons nodded. "Should work just fine. Not sure what the problem was earlier, but you shouldn't have any more trouble with that critter. Watch your back, eh?"

"Always." Shaun turned his attention back to Lexie as the head of security left the room. "Ready to move out? You can still change your mind. Whoever set the gas in the library is still out there, and they may try again."

"And I say, you can remind me about the danger all you want, but it's not going to change my mind." She reached back to adjust her hair clip, pulling more of her midlength brown locks up off her shoulders. "There's never a good enough reason to give up on finding someone. No matter how long it takes."

Lexie couldn't read the look Shaun gave her, but

she didn't have time to think it over—he pulled an object from his pocket and handed it to her.

"Switchblade," he said, taking it back from her open palm and flicking it open. He closed it and returned it to her hand. "I grabbed it from my room on the way back from checking out the library for evidence. It's no snazzy gadget, but it might come in handy if you're caught by surprise. Keep it in your pocket or the instep of your shoe, somewhere accessible if you're grabbed."

Lexie tried to give it back to him. "I've taken plenty of self-defense courses. I don't want to use a weapon, and I'm not sure I can."

"You can if your life is in danger. Promise me you'll use it."

As much as she didn't want to accept the blade, having a sharp tool around did make sense. If either of them had had this while they were in the library, they might have been able to unscrew the bolts on the door or slide the blade underneath to cut the tape. "If necessity calls for it, I will use it."

"Promise?"

He clearly had no intention of letting her out of the room without a promise. Lexie slipped the switchblade into her pocket and patted it. "Promise," she said, backing toward the door. "But if I have to carry something, I'd prefer a Walther PPK."

She enjoyed the look of incredulity on his face

at her reference to the fictional superspy James Bond's weapon of choice. The surprise morphed into a grin as he hurried after her.

Lexie followed Shaun in silence from the medical center as they did their best not to wake any sleeping passengers in the surrounding cabins. Most passengers had settled in for the night, though they passed a few bleary-eyed stragglers who looked as though they had no intention of sleeping on an icebound ship. Upon reaching a key-operated maintenance elevator, Shaun pulled Parsons's key from his pocket and called up the car.

The elevator car clanged and creaked as the cables drew it up to their floor. For some reason, the silence between them felt awkward in a way it hadn't before their shared moment in the library. Lexie blamed herself. She couldn't deny there'd been a charge in the air when they'd stood too close together, but admittedly she could have leaped away with less enthusiasm when trouble started. "Are we sure that's safe?"

Shaun grimaced at the screech of the opening doors but showed no sign of being perturbed by their unrequited shelving encounter. Had she read too much into the moment?

And why couldn't she stop thinking about it?

"I'll check it out," he said, stepping into the

small elevator car. The maintenance elevator floor space was only about five feet by five feet, wide enough to fit a broken dishwasher, a medical gurney or a folded cot. Lexie winced as Shaun jumped in place twice. When the car didn't go crashing down into the basement of the ship, he swept a hand across to invite her in. "After you, Miss Reilly."

Lexie peered into the elevator, noting its dingy, exposed lightbulb and tarnished handrails. "Remind me again why we have to search the lower decks?"

The corner of Shaun's mouth curled upward and he backed into the far corner of the elevator. "You're welcome to hang out with the captain if you're having second thoughts."

"Not a chance." Lexie stepped inside the elevator and flinched at the coldness of the handrail on her warm skin. "If someone wants me out of the way, I'd rather have you nearby than ferry security. No offense to them, but I suspect a superspy is better trained in fending off trouble."

Shaun punched a few buttons on the control panel and the elevator squealed back to life, dropping a few sudden inches before continuing its descent. "I'm not a superspy, Lexie. Far from it. I'm just a man trying to make the world a better place in the best way I can. I don't always succeed, either."

She couldn't help it—an unladylike snort escaped as his words sunk in. "Sorry, I'm allergic to clichés."

"I'm serious." Shaun looked wounded, but Lexie didn't buy it.

"You're trying to make the world a better place by hiding in the shadows?"

"You call what we're doing right now hiding in the shadows?"

"I call you planning to tackle some ridiculously dangerous trafficking ring on your own without a lick of help 'hiding in the shadows,' yes. If I hadn't been attacked and you hadn't been there, no one else on board would know and you'd be doing this all alone."

Shaun widened his stance as the elevator slowed. "Just like you were when you came on board in search of a missing girl, by yourself and unarmed?"

"I didn't anticipate that anyone would be trying to kill me."

"Now you can see why I might not want to reveal my identity and purpose to just anyone."

She did see, yes. And it made perfect sense. Why was she trying to antagonize him? No, wrong question. She knew exactly why. Holding on to anger and resentment was so much easier than shifting her perspective, especially when it meant admitting that her sister had lied after all.

Because that would mean that Shaun wasn't the villain she'd made him out to be, and that in turn meant she just might be tempted to risk her heart.

The elevator reached its destination, jerking into place with several high-pitched screeches. As much as Shaun wanted to continue this line of conversation—specifically to find out why she'd suddenly decided to condemn his career choice— the important thing right now was to keep moving. The longer they stayed in one place, the more likely it'd be that their attacker would find and surprise them. *Again.*

In Shaun's experience, killers whose plans failed to kill their intended target tended to feel desperate and become unpredictable. While the mantra often cited during training said that desperate people tended to make more mistakes, those mistakes usually came at a cost for everyone involved— perp and victim. Shaun would not let that happen to Lexie. Not today, not ever. But despite having read psych profile after psych profile on the Wolf, the truth was that no one had yet been able to determine a pattern of behavior for the man. He seemed to use whatever resources were available to him, with a whole army of lackeys firmly entrenched across North America and elsewhere to do his dirty work. Whoever the man was, he'd kept his hands clean for too long. Shaun was ready to see them coated in grime.

"There's a storage room to the left, and the engine room to the right. Parsons said there's another storage area in the engine room, mostly with parts and grease, that kind of thing, but we'll check there last since it's going to be the most complicated area to navigate. I'd rather not bother the guys working in there if we don't have to. Our goal is to identify if anything is missing, specifically anything on this list." He handed Lexie a sticky note listing the ingredients and supplies needed to create and deliver hydrogen sulfide through a tube. "If you see anything strange—a circle in the dust, a cap askew on a jug, anything at all—say something. Two sets of eyes are better than one."

"Got it." She managed to get one foot out of the elevator before Shaun grabbed her shoulder and pulled her back inside. She glared at him in annoyance. "What now?"

"Let me take point. I know you don't want to, but humor me on this, okay? I doubt our culprit will be down here, but I'd feel more comfortable playing lookout." He pressed a hand to his side, an automatic habit to check for the position of his gun. "If I were him, I'd be upstairs trying to blend in with the other passengers."

Lexie raised her palms in surrender. "Whatever you say, Captain Superdude."

He winced at the mash-up superhero reference. Far from being the compliment she'd intended, being called a superhero took on an entirely different meaning for Shaun. Being a superhero tended to get people killed, and frankly he couldn't think of a superhero from comics or television who had it all together. Sure, superheroes helped others and saved the world, but they did it while neglecting the needs of the people closest to them. Having two identities made it tough to be there for loved ones while saving the universe from certain destruction.

He'd learned that the hard way. Not a day went by when Shaun didn't wonder if he'd lost the chance for love out of selfish focus on helping others for his own glory. One more corrupt government toppled, three more cancelled dinners. He'd given every part of himself to the cause of national security, and left nothing for the relationships in his life. Eight years after deciding this is what he wanted to do with his life, and he still went home to an empty house after each mission. He'd be lying if he said it didn't get lonely sometimes, but finding the right person who understood the importance of the work he did and how much he believed in it was no easy task.

Besides, after meeting Nikki, Shaun had vowed not to become romantically involved with a woman until he felt capable of balancing his priorities.

While he still wasn't certain if he'd grown ready to take a chance on love, he'd be lying to himself if he said that something about Lexie didn't make him want to try.

To do that, he'd need to leave the "superhero" side of himself behind, and focus on being the best agent and protector he could possibly be. If that included putting himself in the potential line of fire, he'd take that risk without hesitation.

"Hello? Earth to the Captain?" Lexie waved a hand in front of his face. "Thought I'd lost you there for a minute."

"Let's hope it never comes to that." Shaun pushed past her and peered out of the elevator, checking up and down the hall. "Clear."

The hallways on the engine room deck were lit by dim yellow caged lightbulbs. Since few people spent time on this deck—aside from working on the engine or performing other mechanical repairs—Shaun recognized the reduced lighting as a cost-saving measure. No passengers had access to this deck, which placed its upkeep low on the list of priorities. As long as all the critical parts of the ship worked, what did some chipped paint and bad lighting matter?

The lack of population on this level, however, made it the perfect place to steal supplies from. Or hide a whole person. The constant rumble of the engine would make it harder to hear someone moving around down here.

They found and searched three storage closets before heading toward the engine room. None of the closets contained anything useful. Shaun noted that Lexie's demeanor became less and less enthusiastic about the search as they went on, but she remained determined. He knew he was falling for that intensity—that fire she'd given him glimpses of. He couldn't deny Lexie's character as a strong, capable woman, but how many times could a person have their life put in danger before they cracked? He'd experienced more than his share of life-threatening moments, but agents had counselors and therapists to talk to after missions. All Lexie had on board was...well, him, and even a strong, capable woman like Lexie could crack under the weight of constant pressure. The more he knew of her, the more of himself he could give to be there for her.

Whether she wanted him to be there for her or not, after living with the belief that he'd crushed her sister's heart and sent her into a life-destroying tailspin, was another question entirely.

"This one's empty," Lexie was saying, after they'd found a little shelving unit inside a staff washroom. "All it holds is toilet paper and soap. And a few old issues of *The Economist*."

Shaun took the magazines from Lexie and

turned them over in his hands. "No address. Bought off the rack. One of our ferry staff must have a strong interest in world affairs." He placed them back on the shelf. "Interesting, but not helpful."

Lexie knocked a fist against her forehead, thinking. "Is it not possible that the person who gassed us brought the supplies with them onto the ship? Maybe they planned ahead."

"In their car, with their kidnapping victim? It's possible, sure. Not likely, but possible. That's another reason we need Reed to find the passenger he caught trying to snoop down here. Even if he's not involved, he may have seen something." Shaun led them out of the washroom and farther down the hall to the heart of the deck. They stopped in front of the engine room, the scent of grease already wafting out through the cracks around the door.

A bold red sign on the door warned visitors to notify the manager on duty of their presence in the room upon arrival. "Safety protocol," Shaun said, knocking on the door. "This is probably the most dangerous room on the ship. Aside from the kitchen," he added with a wink.

Lexie's frozen exterior showed a crack as she released a hint of a smile. "Very funny. I'd like to see you try cooking for hundreds of people at once, every day."

"How about just for one?" He grinned at her and turned his attention back to the door. When no one answered his knock, he tried the door handle and, finding it unlocked, swung the door open. He knocked again on the door frame and called into the room.

Lexie peered around him into the red-orange glow. "Hey, with the ferry stopped by the ice, does anyone even need to be down here? And why is there so much noise?"

Shaun pointed to one well-lit unit in the far corner of the room, resisting the urge to engage her in a conversation about home cooking. And dinners together. *Focus. This is no time for distractions.* "One thing at a time, Reilly. The engine room still needs manpower because we're still using electricity, even if we're not going anywhere. No propulsion, sure, but we still have to power the lights. And the ovens." He paused and called into the room, "Hello? Anybody home?"

He and Lexie stepped carefully into the room. The gloomy, reddish glow of the emergency exit lights gave the place a spooky vibe. Beside him, Lexie shivered.

"You all right?" He clutched his vest, ready to offer it to her if she needed it.

She shook her head. "I don't like this. Where are all the staff? If we really are still using all this power—"

The door slammed behind them and they both spun around. As Lexie shouted in surprise, Shaun had just enough time to register the shape of a man flying toward them out of the shadows.

NINE

Instinctively, Shaun wrapped his arms around Lexie and pushed them both over, spinning into a sideways roll to soften their fall. He continued the roll and released her. With Lexie safely behind him, Shaun leaped to his feet just in time for a poorly aimed uppercut to clip the side of his jaw. Shaun cushioned the blow by moving instinctively with the punch.

It hurt like crazy, but Shaun managed to keep enough of his wits about him to see the wrench that came swinging up toward his skull from the left. He ducked, reached up to grab the man's arm and flipped the attacker onto his back.

The man rolled away, scrambled to his feet and reached for something in his belt. Shaun's hopes sank, and he prayed that Lexie had enough sense to run for it while she still could.

"We just want to talk to you," Shaun yelled, hoping to stall the man from doing what he feared.

"We're not going to hurt you. We're only looking for—"

A deafening blast echoed throughout the room, and a sudden pressure on Shaun's shoulder dropped him to the floor. He grabbed his shoulder and his fingers came away wet and sticky. A burning sensation, like a bee sting, crawled across his skin. A woman's scream brought him back to his senses. *Lexie.* "Run, Lexie. Get out of here!"

Another blast brought a second scream, and a third blast was followed by silence. Shaun's heart tightened. Why hadn't the gunman finished him off? *Where there's hesitation, there's hope.*

He reached into his waistband for his gun as footsteps banged across the floor. Before Shaun could raise his weapon, a steel-toed boot swung through the air and smashed into his fingers, sending his gun skidding across the floor. It disappeared into the shadows around the room's machinery. *So much for hope.*

"Do you really want to kill us?" Shaun decided to try a different tactic and prayed that God would give him the right words to say. This assailant couldn't be the Wolf, because the Wolf wouldn't have missed his shot. That meant this person had to be a lackey, and lackeys could be persuaded. "We can help you. Or you can use us as leverage. Doesn't your boss want to talk to us, find out what we know?"

Shaun struggled to prop himself up on one elbow. The burning in his shoulder was intensifying by the second, and his damp shirt clung to his skin. He forced himself to look up into the eyes of the man in front of him—but instead found his gaze focused on the barrel of a gun pointed at his forehead.

The gun shook in the hands of the man holding it, a man of average build and height, wearing a black Atlantic Voyages uniform. *The man from the parking deck!* Sweat stuck long strands of dirty blond hair to the man's forehead, as though he'd been sitting in this room premeditating the encounter for some time. Had he heard Shaun and Lexie searching and waited for the right time to strike?

"You…you can't be here," the man stammered. "My boss doesn't need to talk to you."

This was good. If Shaun kept the man talking, he'd have time to figure out a plan. "Why not? Doesn't he want our intel? To know who we report to and what we know?"

The man's eyes widened, but he shook his head, the gun trembling violently in his hand. Shaun prayed that the tremor wouldn't cause an accidental discharge before he had a chance to talk the man down. Every second the barrel remained pointed at his forehead reduced the chances of

Lexie and him getting out of the room alive. If she was even…

No. He refused to entertain that thought.

They needed to get out of here, fast.

"He…already knows all that," the man replied. His eyes darted around the room and back to Shaun. "And he told me your services are no longer required."

As the man finished speaking, a glint of light illuminated the edge of the switchblade Shaun had given Lexie, just before Lexie plunged it into the gunman's leg from behind. Shaun rolled out of the way an instant before a bullet exploded from the gun. He scrambled to his feet while the man in front of him screeched in pain.

"Go, Lexie!" Shaun motioned for her to move, to get out of the room and out of the way. They were still in danger. "Get upstairs and get help!"

But instead of running, Shaun's pleas stirred Lexie into action. A wave of resolution rolled across her face as she leaped forward and wrapped her arms around the gunman's neck, giving Shaun the opening he needed to grab their attacker's wrist and knock his gun away. It skidded away just like Shaun's weapon had, sliding underneath one of the engine room's massive machines.

But all weapons weren't out of play yet, which their attacker realized at the same moment it dawned on Shaun. Despite Lexie's firm grip on the man's neck, he strained against the pressure, reaching down to yank the switchblade out of his leg before Shaun could grab it. When Shaun moved in to try and retrieve the blade, the man reared his head back and slammed it forward.

Their skulls collided and Shaun fell backward, pain blossoming in his forehead to match that in his shoulder. The world spun, and he could barely make out the scene in front of him.

And then his vision cleared and he saw it. The man had Lexie in a choke hold, switchblade against her throat.

Blood pooled around the knife's tip.

"Not so confident now, hmm?" The man's voice shook. "I should get a promotion for this."

Lexie took shallow breaths, feeling a trickle of blood as it trailed down the side of her neck. The bruises on her throat from the parking deck encounter throbbed from the stress of the moment, but even more disturbing was the lack of pain from the knife at her throat. Shaun's blade was incredibly sharp—if this man chose to end her life with it, he'd be able to do it quickly and efficiently. Making a wrong move would sink the blade into her throat like butter.

From the floor, Shaun groaned, though he didn't move. Relief washed over Lexie that he was still alive—but with Shaun incapacitated, the ball fell in her court to get them out in one piece. She tried to recall her basic self-defense training, but each scenario risked too much. The attacker's unsteady grip on the knife made him unpredictable and very, very dangerous.

"You don't want to do this," Lexie whispered, mind racing for the right words to say. "There's no way out without getting caught. The authorities have been searching for you for a long time. Let us go, and we'll put in a good word to the police. We're more use to you alive than dead."

"Me? They don't want me, but I want you." The man slurred his words, his voice shaking. "Not gonna kill you, lady. Only have permission to take the man out. What am I gonna do with you until the boss gets here?"

Lexie's heartbeat sped up as the man muttered to himself. This wasn't the Wolf. One of his gang? Maybe she could use this information to her advantage. "You don't have permission to kill me? That's odd, considering your boss tried to kill me twice already."

The man laughed, hysteria causing his vocal pitch to rise and fall in frenzy. "You think so, yes? Of course. Of course you do."

The knife tip bit into Lexie's neck as the man laughed, his arms shaking. *Now* she felt the edge of the blade. Panic rose in her belly, but she clamped it down. She *could not* have a panic attack here.

Instead, she pressed herself back farther into her attacker's body to avoid an accident from his trembling knife hand. He stunk like sweat and grease, and Lexie suppressed the urge to gag. Orders or not, if either of them made a wrong move, it'd be game over.

"Who's your boss? Can you tell me that?" She willed Shaun to wake up, but he hadn't moved an inch since falling to the floor after that head butt. What if he needed a hospital? "We can help you out of this. You don't want to be a killer."

"My boss? He'll tell you when he gets here." The man sniffed. "Gotta call him, tell him to get down here."

"Isn't he already on his way?"

"Shut up." The man spat into her ear, flecks of spittle landing on her neck. "Maybe, maybe not. Gotta call him, tell him the...the intrusion has been dealt with."

That meant he'd have to either release his grip on her arms or the knife at her neck to make the call. She could use that, provided he didn't think to incapacitate her before doing so. He certainly didn't seem capable of rational thought at the moment, and with the gun out of play, she might actually have a chance.

Lexie formulated a visual plan. If she could stomp on his instep and free an arm to push the knife away at the same time, she might avoid the blade going through her jugular. But she'd have to wait until his attention shifted to calling his boss. What about Shaun? She regarded his prone figure. If she got away, what would stop this madman from taking out Shaun permanently while she called for help? And how would she find help before the Wolf found *her*?

Thinking about that only complicated things. Better to act and do it soon, and figure out the next step from there. If she didn't get medical attention to Shaun in time, she'd never forgive herself.

Her next glance at Shaun sent a wave of relief flooding through her body. He looked at her through the slit of one eyelid and shook his head subtly—just enough for her to get the message. *Don't try anything stupid.*

"You need a walkie-talkie?" Lexie asked, an idea forming. The idea risked much, but so did doing nothing.

The man stopped muttering and his trembling arm froze. "Yeah. Yeah, I do. But it's in the back and you'll try some funny business if I let you go."

"What about the one he has?" Lexie hoped that Shaun would take her cues. "He's got a radio that we were using earlier. Not sure if the batteries are still working, but checking means you can keep me in front of you so I can't try anything."

The man remained silent for a few seconds

before the pressure of the knife against her neck eased. "Yeah, good. That works."

He pushed her along in front of him, crossing to where Shaun lay. Lexie hoped Shaun had recovered enough of his senses and strength to make this worthwhile. Once they reached Shaun's body, her attacker knelt and pulled her down with him, leaning forward so that he could use his bottom hand to reach the walkie-talkie on Shaun's belt.

Right on cue, Shaun sprang to life. He grabbed the man's knife hand and twisted, sending the switchblade clattering to the ground. Lexie reeled backward and smashed the back of her head into the man's face. A sickening crunch told her she'd aimed well. His nose would be pouring blood in seconds, which gave her an opening to dive for the knife as Shaun pinned the man's arms and gathered him into a choke hold.

"Chair, rope," Shaun said to Lexie, his breath heavy from the exertion. "Let's get him secured and get out of here."

Lexie couldn't believe her ears. "We're just going to leave him here? Shouldn't we bring him upstairs?"

"Bring a bloody, sweating engineer onto the passenger decks, where tensions are already high?"

"Good point."

"And I'm afraid the Wolf might already be on his

way. Whoever is doing this seems to know where we are at all times, so I'd rather not stick around."

Lexie shook her head. "He said he had to call his boss. That implies that this time he doesn't know, doesn't it?"

"You really want to take that chance?"

Of course she didn't. "Did you hear what he said, though? He didn't have permission to kill me, only you. What do you think that means?"

"I think we're dealing with people who will lie and deceive in order to get their way." Shaun grunted, tightening his hold on their assailant. "I don't recommend being quick to believe everything they say to you. It's a tactic kidnappers sometimes use to put their victims at ease."

Lexie shivered at the thought of what might have happened, trying to push it from her mind and replace it with relief that they'd both come out of the attack alive. Seeing Shaun down and immobile had brought unwelcome feelings to the surface, feelings that suggested she'd grown to care about this man far more than she should in the past twelve hours. How could he have such an effect on her so quickly? Yes, the man had good looks—and plenty of them—but that was secondary to his care, kindness and dedication to his cause.

Could it be that she felt drawn to their commonalities? His protector drive certainly complemented her "go get 'em" approach to the search.

But that's where it had to end. She had no desire for a relationship, and moreover not one with *him*.

Lexie found a chair in the far corner and grabbed a coil of rope from a pile at the back of the room. When she returned with both items, Shaun plunked their now-unconscious assailant in the chair.

"What'd you do?" Lexie gaped at him. "Was that necessary?"

"If we don't want him to scream and fight us as we're securing him, then yes. Don't worry, it wasn't painful. I didn't hurt him further, if that's what you're thinking."

"Sure you didn't."

Shaun held up his hands, finally freed of needing to hold on to their attacker. "Honest. You learn this kind of stuff in spy school."

"Spy school?" Lexie couldn't tell if he was teasing her or not. "That's a real thing?"

"Of course it is. Rope, please." He grinned as she tossed the rope, but he got down to business the moment it reached his hands. How could he joke around at a time like this? It reminded her of the Shaun she and her sister had met all those years ago in dusty Africa, teenaged Shaun with a penchant for practical jokes and razzing on authority. Some things about people never changed. Others did. He seemed so sure of himself now, confident in his decisions and capable of doing what needed to be done without hesitation. During their short time together on this ferry, he'd known exactly what to say to diffuse the tension of the moment and make her feel safe with him. Still, Nikki's accusations played on repeat in the back of her mind.

"Have you tied up prisoners before?" she asked, only partially serious. "You seem to know what you're doing."

He chuckled, tugged on an end of rope, and stepped back to survey his work. "You know how it is in this line of work. You don't even get a locker until you've passed Rope Tying 101." He winked at her, then looked over her head toward the door. "Let's leave him here and go find Parsons. I don't want to be around without backup if the Wolf decides to check up on his ally, and maybe they've tracked down that passenger by now."

Lexie shivered at the thought of being caught by surprise by the ringleader. "He had a gun, Shaun. Do you think that means his boss has one, too? Brought one on board?"

"I'd be a fool to rule it out," he said, voice soft. He crossed the room and brushed back a lock of hair that had escaped from her hairclip during the scuffle. "So I won't. But there's no need for panic. We've got one of his allies subdued, and we've taken out one possible weapons threat. We need to call this a win."

He squeezed her shoulder, and the muscles in Lexie's stomach tensed and relaxed. It *was* a win. They'd come through this alive, and now they had a direct line to the Wolf—someone who could provide them with information on Maria and her captor.

The realization brought with it a wave of relief, followed by exhaustion. After the events of the last twelve hours, she desperately needed a hug. Simple as that. Shaun just so happened to be the closest available candidate. He responded to her hug in kind, offering a secure but gentle embrace. And yet, when neither of them let go, the moment shifted to something more.

Shaun kissed the top Lexie's head and her body betrayed her, shivering in response.

It felt right, but in other ways, oh so wrong. She swallowed, knowing what she needed to say next. "Shaun, I can't. This can't be." Lexie waved at the man tied to the chair. "Look at where we are, at what's happening. Plus, you've told me my sister lied to me about what happened between the two of you. I've spent so much time blaming you for sending her off the deep end that I can't just erase everything I believed in a matter of hours."

Shaun nodded, but there was no mistaking the disappointment in his eyes. He pulled away and held her at arm's length, hands on her shoulders. Her body wanted to close the gap and feel the security of his embrace again, but her brain overruled her on this one. Solve the problem, decide if he'd told her the truth and go from there. Whatever that meant.

Shaun cleared his throat, breaking the stillness between them. "As nice as this is, we need to move. The Wolf is coming."

TEN

Shaun's pulse raced, and it had nothing to with the gunshot wound, skull trauma or having caught one of the Wolf's lackeys. Lying on the floor, Shaun had praised God to realize that the bullet to his shoulder had only grazed it. He'd lost a lot of blood, but not enough to put his health or mobility at risk. Lexie's quick thinking had saved the day, enabling him to fight through the pain and execute her on-the-spot plan.

Being this close to Lexie…it did a number on him, that's for sure. The sensation of her arms around him was both wonderful and welcome, though at first, he'd held back from assuming what it meant. How many hugs had he received from grateful victims he'd helped save throughout the years? But then neither he nor she had pulled away, and he didn't want to be the first to let go.

She fit so well in his arms. Like two puzzle pieces, made for each other—but not only that, they understood each other better than anyone he'd ever met. He'd had plenty of partners in the field on missions before who wouldn't have thought to trick their captor the way she did, psychologically influencing the man who'd put her in mortal danger and using teamwork to take him down without further injury.

And as much as he wanted to relish the moment she'd given him, getting to safety before the Wolf found them took priority. They'd return with Parsons's team to get some answers from their captive, relying on safety in numbers. *Then* he could tell Lexie about the static charge that filled the air every time she came near.

"Let's take the maintenance elevator back up," Lexie suggested as they left the engine room. "That way we can land on the correct floor without interference, right? And if we can get in touch with security, maybe those guys can meet us right at the top and we can come straight down again."

"Solid planning," Shaun said, impressed yet again by her forward thinking. No wonder she'd worked her way up to vice president at the missing-persons organization. She possessed the perfect blend of logic, fire and compassion required by such an emotionally demanding job. It was clear that the search for Maria was far more than just another job for Lexie. She cared about the young woman and her family, and Shaun didn't blame her one bit. Was that why she hadn't yet married? He knew all about the difficulties inherent in this kind of work. Leaving it at the office wasn't exactly an option.

They stepped into the elevator as Shaun tried to contact Parsons on the walkie-talkie, but the thick metal walls that lined the elevator shaft made it difficult for the signal to get through. "Hello? Hey, Parsons?" Shaun tried to adjust the reception, and a faint voice came through the static as the elevator reached the lounge deck. "I can't get him from inside here. Let's get to an open space and try to call again."

After several additional tries, the radio's alert tone sounded for an incoming call. "Lane here."

"Lane? Parsons. You looking for me?" The man's voice sounded strained, but Shaun figured he'd be feeling the strain, too, if he had to take care of an entire ferry's worth of irate passengers. For the sake of the entire *MV Providence* staff, he hoped the icebreaker ship arrived soon.

"We had a situation in the engine room," Shaun explained. "Lexie and I took care of it, and we're safe. Mostly unharmed." He decided not to bore the man with details on the continuing throb from the gunshot graze on his shoulder, the massive headache from having his skull bashed and the heavy sensation still in his lungs from the gas incident. And the cut on Lexie's neck. "We need your help, though. Can your team meet us at the south passenger elevators on the main deck in three? The maintenance elevator is probably too small for all of us, now that I think of it. I want to move as a group on this one. We were two against one and still had a close call. I'm not keen on taking another unnecessary risk. Bring a few bandages and some iodine if you can."

The walkie-talkie grew silent, and Shaun wondered if Parsons's battery had died. The man's voice returned over the speaker just as Shaun had decided to head to one of the ship's little convenience stalls and commandeer some batteries.

"South passenger elevators, main deck, First Aid, three minutes. Roger."

Shaun clipped the walkie-talkie back onto his belt, noting that Lexie had stopped near a window. She stared outside into the darkness, her expression guarded. He hadn't noticed until now, but her eyelids were heavy and dark circles had begun to form under her eyes. What had he been thinking, dragging her around on a search in the middle of the night? She hadn't said one word of protest though and had taken everything in stride. Despite the woman's immense strength and patience, he'd allowed her to be put in the line of fire one too many times.

"You should get some rest," he commented. "You look exhausted."

Her lips turned downward in a delicate frown,

and he mentally kicked himself. *Wrong choice of words, genius.*

"Thanks. I'm sure you've looked better, yourself." She squinted and stepped closer. "You know you've got blood all over your shirt, right?"

"Just a flesh wound," he quipped.

"Right." Lexie rolled her eyes and flicked a finger at his walkie-talkie. "We take care of the situation downstairs and then you get to medical."

"Only if you get some actual rest. In a real bed, with a guard posted."

"Aren't the staff stretched thin enough as it is?"

Shaun pressed his lips together and exhaled. "I meant me."

"And you'll sleep when?"

"When this is over and everyone is safe." Before she could argue, he placed a hand on her shoulder and directed her down the hallway, back toward the passenger elevators. "Come on. We've got a minute to get back there to meet Parsons, and a guy tied up in the engine room."

Never a dull moment, he thought as they turned the corner to the elevator hallway. Standing alone in front of the doors was security team member Josh.

Josh held a weapon in his hands, and he had it aimed at Lexie.

Shaun grabbed Lexie's shoulder and pulled her behind him, blocking her body with his own.

"Hold on," Shaun said, trying to keep his voice calm and steady. "I thought we were on the same side."

Confusion followed by relief played across Josh's face, and he lowered the weapon. He holstered it, allowing Shaun a glimpse of the object. A stun gun. Not a gun with bullets, but just as painful and potentially deadly. Did all the security staff have them?

Josh held up his empty hands. "Sorry. Getting a little jumpy is all. I got punched in the stomach by a passenger a half hour ago when I told him we're almost out of bacon in the restaurant."

"Bacon?" Shaun came forward slowly, keeping Lexie behind him. "Is that in your job description, updating passengers on the availability of their buffet options?"

Josh chuckled and pressed the call button for the elevator. Creaking and grinding came from within the elevator shaft as the car made its way to their floor. "No, but you try telling a guest that they can't devour two pounds of bacon because there are other people aboard who need to eat, too, and no way to get more food until we hit shore. The guy seemed to think we could just call a helicopter to bring in another pig. Have it land on the ice or throw packages of bacon onto the top of the ship. Or send it in by parachute, I don't know."

As weird as it sounded, Shaun believed him.

People tended to act strange when afraid, even if the fear wasn't entirely rational. "Did you tell him you'd be happy to hire a door-to-door helicopter bacon delivery service if he paid for it?"

Josh lifted the corner of his shirt, where a massive red welt had swollen on his abdomen. "Naturally. And he showed me exactly what he thought of the suggestion. Huh. Maintenance really needs to spray some WD-40 on these passenger elevators, eh?"

"Compared to the maintenance elevators, this is a symphony." The noisy elevator came to a stop, doors opening. To Shaun's surprise, Parsons and Reed were already inside. "Got a head start on the ride, did you?"

Parsons stepped back, making room for the three waiting persons to board. "We were still on the upper decks, figured it'd be faster to meet up this way. Reed thinks he's found our trespasser, too, for what it's worth. The guy entered room sixty-five about ten minutes ago. Won't be hard to check the manifest and page him to the office once we're done with this business. Or we can just haul him out of bed, whatever works. Coming?"

Shaun shot a glance at Lexie, who offered him a brief, encouraging smile. Finding the passenger was extremely good news—they just might have earned two solid leads in under an hour. Gaining any solid intel from either of the two men could blow three years of guesswork and baby steps wide open, and save Maria's life in the meantime.

They boarded the elevator and descended in silence to the engine deck. Shaun led the way to the engine room, Lexie close beside him. In any other circumstance, he'd be enjoying her nearness. Right now, seeing the exhaustion and paranoia plain on her face, he wondered if he shouldn't have left her upstairs in the medical center.

"We tied up the man who attacked us," Shaun said, addressing the other men as they reached the door. "It's a little old-school, but it worked. He was unconscious when we left, but should be awake by now. I didn't put him out for long." Shaun sensed, rather than saw, Lexie's eyes roll behind him.

Parsons nodded, a gesture of understanding between two professionals, despite their different positions and levels of service. Shaun had worked plenty of field and recon assignments where he and his team had gone head-to-head with local law enforcement, and it always made everyone's jobs that much harder. As much as he'd complained earlier to Jack about working with a couple of security guards on this highly sensitive case, Parsons had displayed nothing but professionalism the entire time. It'd certainly help to have Parsons backing him up in the inevitable police investigation once they reached Argentia. He'd have to buy the man dinner to say thanks, maybe ask why he'd gone into the security business over a law enforcement career.

"Is this our guy?" Parsons asked, crossing his arms. "The one you briefed us on?"

"One of them." Shaun braced his shoulder against the door, half-turned with his attention on the rest of the group. "Not the Wolf, but our attacker mentioned having a boss. Once we get in here, it's my job to confirm that boss's identity. You three take point around the room and ensure we're not ambushed. Lexie sticks with me." He nodded acknowledgment to each man in turn, ensuring they'd understood his instructions. "I doubt his boss will be willing to take on a group of five, or at least that's what I'm counting on. This shouldn't take long."

Shaun pushed the door open, holding it in place with his shoulder as he turned around to face the room—and froze.

Lexie's small frame bumped into him from behind, followed by a grunt of annoyance from one of the other men.

"Don't move," Shaun said, keeping his voice low and steady. "Parsons, come around. Don't let Lexie—"

"No way, buddy." Lexie pushed past him to see into the room and immediately let out a cry of horror. Shaun grabbed her arm and pulled her tight into his chest, covering her face.

The man they'd left tied up still sat on the chair, about ten feet from the door. Blood covered the man's body and the floor around the chair, with a scarlet red trail leading to a clear message written on the engine room floor. *WHO'S NEXT?*

Lexie shook, her whole body trembling as Shaun held her upright. Her legs felt weak and rubbery, and though she closed her eyes to block out the memory, all she saw behind her eyelids was the disturbing, horrifying image of their bloodied attacker tied to the chair.

And the message. Who would write such a thing? No one but a cold-blooded killer—someone who didn't care one whit for humanity, who saw people as commodities to be bought and sold—could craft such a disturbing scene. If this man, this Wolf, was willing to kill his own associates, what else would he do to protect his interests?

"My stomach," Lexie mumbled, waves of nausea and heat washing over her from head to toe. "Shaun…"

Shaun held her at arm's length. "Should we get you a bucket? I know that sounds insensitive, but I don't want to send you to a washroom alone."

She took a deep breath through her nose and swallowed down the bile that rose in her throat. This would make poor timing for a panic attack, but she felt sick to her stomach more than anything. "I'm not sure. Give me a minute." The question she didn't want answered leaped unbidden from her lips. "Is he dead?"

Shaun sighed and glanced over her head. She knew what that meant.

Inside the engine room, the security men were arguing about protocol. She'd let them handle it. For once, she didn't need to be a part of this. "Should we call the Coast Guard? Or radio the police, or... I guess you are the police. Sort of. Right?" She clamped her lips together to stop rambling, but the motion did nothing to stop the rest of her body from trembling as guilt tumbled onto her conscience like a bag of bricks. "What if we hadn't left him here? What if we'd just taken him upstairs, or—"

Shaun took her chin in his hand, forcing her to meet his gaze. "Stop. There are no what-ifs, here. The man who did this is willing to go to extreme lengths to protect his interests, and no speculation on what we could have done will change that."

"But I don't understand. Why kill someone who's helping you? Why not just untie him and help him hide or have him come after us again?"

Shaun sighed again, heavier this time and released her chin. Lexie wished he hadn't. The warmth of his touch had helped to steady her nerves, though guiltily she couldn't help but wonder if he'd led Nikki on with similar gentle embraces and caring gestures. Couldn't her sister ever stay out of her thoughts?

"Information," Shaun said. "And to send a warning. It's possible he assumed the man talked when we captured him, or he saw the man as a weak link in his operation. This is a message about interference, since we didn't heed the first one."

"But…who's *next*?" Lexie clutched her middle, feeling the acid of the coffee and lack of food roiling around in her insides. How long had it been since her last meal? How long since she'd slept? It felt as if she'd driven her car onto the ferry's parking deck a week ago. "What does he mean? Is he talking about us?"

Shaun's throat bobbed as he swallowed and broke eye contact with Lexie. He knew something he didn't want to tell her, and she recognized that look. He had seen this before. How was that possible? How could a person see this kind of thing over and over and not lose their mind?

Or, on the other hand, how could he see such horrible things over and over again and not be *changed*?

ELEVEN

This changed everything. Shaun held Lexie tight, sheltering her from the gruesome scene as he fought to control his own emotions. Anger threatened to consume him, the temptation to give in to its destructive power nearly overwhelming. With this promising lead on the Wolf gone, time was running out faster than ever. This man had purposefully shown them his willingness to kill to protect his operation. If Shaun and Lexie's investigation led them too close, who could say whether the Wolf wouldn't take the life of his current captive if it meant preventing his entire operation's exposure?

For the past three years of this mission, CIA intel had tagged the Wolf simply as a clever but dangerous trafficker who moved people as cargo across land and sea. The man's operation posed a threat to the daughters, cousins and mothers of the United States and elsewhere, and he'd stayed one step ahead of Shaun and the Agency this whole time. Shaun had pegged this as part coincidence and part intelligent strategy.

But with one look at the bloodied man before him, Shaun had to change his entire perspective. The Wolf had revealed himself as a true murderer under pressure—staying one step ahead through fear and violence. If that kind of violence could be applied to the people the Wolf worked with en route, it also had to include the women in his care.

Shaun had seen this kind of thing only once before, when he'd come within a hairsbreadth of catching the man in Spain. Shaun's team had extracted everyone—captives, accomplices, civilians who hadn't known any better—except for one person. That one person had been left, just like this, to send Shaun's team a message…but they'd never been able to definitively prove it as the Wolf's handiwork. Still, that death had been one death too many. This second one threatened to make Shaun blind and livid with rage at the absolute waste of life.

Shaun glanced over at the scene again. It had been a messy, disrespectful way to end anyone's life, criminal or not. The only good to come out of this was the knowledge that they had to be close. No one disposed of an ally unless they were desperate, which meant they had their target running scared.

While Shaun wished he could help Lexie un-see

the scene before them, the stark truth of the matter was that Shaun's three-year operation to take this man down—and save hundreds, if not thousands of lives—could be coming to a close.

The awareness of this truth sent a ripple of determined excitement through Shaun, which lasted until the moment he looked down at the woman in his arms. She'd asked him a question and now gazed up at him with wide, red-rimmed eyes, tears slipping down her cheeks even as she set her jaw in resolve. She was struggling to stay strong, but a scene like this would shake anyone, regardless of their experience or constitution. It was only a stomach like iron that kept him upright at a moment like this. He longed to kiss each tear away if it meant erasing the image seared onto her eyes.

Lexie had asked him who the message referred to, but he didn't want to answer. He couldn't bear to be the one causing her any more fear. Honestly, Shaun believed it could refer to anyone who'd been involved in this ship-wide search since yesterday evening, but considering the bulk of attacks had focused on Lexie thus far—regardless of whether or not the Wolf actually wanted her dead, despite what their attacker had claimed—Shaun couldn't deny that she had to be in the greatest danger of all.

Back in the medical bay, Lexie watched from her gurney as a nurse cleaned and stitched Shaun's bullet wound. With his back to her, she observed how muscled and strong he really was, though several wide, jagged scars sliced across an otherwise pristine surface. He'd given her the impression of a man fully dedicated to his job, and every so often she'd caught a glimpse of sadness on his face when he thought no one was looking. Still, she'd never fault someone like him for being too devoted to his work. If anything, she understood and felt the same way about her own career choice.

She struggled to find the right words to say, to communicate with him after what she'd seen downstairs. They'd come here together in silence after Shaun chatted briefly with Parsons and his team in the engine room, Shaun only telling her that the other men would take care of things while he kept to his word and got checked out by the nurse. He hadn't said a word to her since.

The nurse finished taping down a bandage to his shoulder, and Lexie waited to speak until she'd disappeared into an adjoining room with another waiting passenger. "Shaun? I'm sorry if I said something wrong." She couldn't imagine what that might have been, but he'd seemed almost angry with her. "I'm just...well, I'm scared. I admit it, I'm scared. I had no idea when I took the reins on Lead Me Home that I'd cause someone to be..."

She ran out of words as Shaun swung his legs around on the gurney, pulling his shirt back on.

He hopped down and leaned against the bed, arms folded across his chest. "It's not your fault a man was killed. You need to understand that. It's no one's fault but the people who've decided that they can treat other human beings like disposable objects."

She shook her head, trying simultaneously to make sense of the scene and erase it from her memory. "He didn't deserve it. No one deserves death, even terrible people."

Shaun took a deep breath and exhaled slowly. "That's one argument, though I know plenty of people who feel differently. As for myself, I prefer justice—real justice. Ultimately, I know that God is the one who brings eternal justice, but it sure would be nice to have some here on earth right about now."

Lexie gaped at him. "Eternal justice? What are you talking about?"

"In the end, God is the only judge who counts. The Bible says—"

"Sorry, I thought we were trying to stop someone from killing an innocent woman, not sit back and wait for some nebulous eternal justice to be dealt out."

"There's nothing nebulous about it. That's what keeps me going, day after day. I can only do so much, Lexie. I have to trust that God will do the rest."

Ire rose in Lexie's gut. How could he talk to her about God with a straight face, after the things he'd done? After the things he'd seen? God didn't care about any of this, because if He did, He'd have kept Nikki away from Shaun in the first place. Maybe Nikki would have participated in the mission trip the way she was supposed to instead of chasing after Shaun, and taken the straight and narrow path to adulthood. Maybe she'd have learned that the world didn't revolve around her after all.

If only Lexie hadn't dragged Nikki along on the mission trip to try and help her in the first place. God of justice? More like God of apathy, if He even cared at all. "You can believe what you want if it makes you feel better, but that's not good enough for me. We need to find this guy and take him down, but on the other hand, if we continue and he's angry, what will that mean for Maria?"

Shaun called the nurse back into the room. "There's no *we* now, Lexie. I'm going to have medical escort you to the captain's quarters. They're vacant at the moment, as the captain has volunteered to take your other room to ensure your safety. His quarters can only be accessed with a new security code known by myself, the captain and the mate. You're going to get some sleep and some food and stay safe until this is over."

Lexie blinked, bewildered by his complete

change of heart. "I thought we were sticking together on this. You agreed."

"I was wrong. I *am* wrong. I've been putting you in extra danger, and that ends here. We've learned that this man is willing to kill, and kill brutally, to get his point across. I will not have you become his next victim."

Lexie hopped off her gurney and stormed across the room to face him, fists balled at her sides. "So that's how this is going to be, huh?"

"What are you talking about?"

"I thought we were partners on this. I thought you and I were, well…"

His expression grew stony and cold. "You thought wrong. If you're ready, I'll take you to the captain's quarters and get you settled. There will be food waiting for you, and if you need anything else, I'll have either the captain or the mate bring it to you."

"Don't you think they have enough to deal with?" she asked flatly.

"They can spare a few minutes for a passenger whose life is in danger. Come on."

He led the way, barely hesitating to ensure she followed behind. And here Lexie had thought she'd finished crying for the day. What had she done wrong to make him act this way? He felt something for her—she was sure of it. And as much as she'd been resisting, she had to stop denying she felt something, too. She didn't like it, but her heart didn't lie.

They walked in silence through the near-empty hallways, most of the passengers now asleep for the night, bellies full of buffet food and minds hopefully quieter despite the ferry's predicament. Shaun introduced her to the captain, who gave her a brief tour of his quarters, complete with attached lounge and kitchenette. They set her up with a pile of blankets and pillows, and a steely-faced Shaun instructed her to lie down and get some sleep.

And then he left, leaving her alone in a strange room, in a strange place, wondering what on earth she'd done to lose him just when she'd been ready to open her heart.

TWELVE

Shaun leaned against the wall outside the captain's quarters. Lexie was right—he *had* promised to keep working together, but that was before someone had been killed. Couldn't she see that? He cared too much for her to continue putting her life at risk.

The alarm sounded on his walkie-talkie, shaking him out of his contemplations. "Tell me we've got something," he said, cutting right to the chase. The faster they resolved this, the better.

"We have a Roger Howard in the office," said Parsons. "Copy of the passenger list for you, too."

"Is he a frequent flier?"

"Eh? He's a repeat visitor, if that's what you mean."

"Great. I'm down the hall, be there in two." Shaun hooked the walkie-talkie back onto his belt and rubbed his tired eyes. Exhaustion had begun to creep up on him, but that might fix itself if this passenger had useful information. Lexie would want to be a part of this, but she desperately needed rest. As much as it pained him to leave her out of it, he knew she'd keep pushing until she collapsed, a trait he understood far too well. He'd also seen the other side of that kind of drive—the despair that came with realizing no matter how many people he saved, there'd always be someone else in danger. To make even a small dent in repairing the world's brokenness demanded sacrifice. Time, relationships, personal hopes and dreams…and until Lexie, he'd emphatically believed that truth. Now?

Now he wondered if that really meant he'd been looking in all the wrong places.

Josh had his head poked out the security office door. He stepped out and shut the door behind him as Shaun approached.

"Here's the list," Josh said, handing Shaun a stapled pile of paper. "Tim had to take care of another passenger crisis, but asked me to get it to you. Gotta say, the snoop isn't thrilled about being hauled down here at this hour."

"He'll be even less thrilled once we start asking questions." Shaun suppressed a yawn. "He's a regular?"

Josh pointed to a highlighted passenger name. "Roger Howard comes through a few times a year. Takes our ferry from North Sydney to Argentia, then heads up the coast to take the Port aux Basques ship back to North Sydney. That one's a six-hour return trip. Times of departure are too close for him to spend any time in Newfoundland."

"Port aux Basques? That's on the southwestern tip, right? Cabot Strait? Some ships were sunk along there by German U-boats during the Second World War."

Josh's eyebrows nearly hit the ceiling. "Someone listened during history class."

Shaun shrugged. "I have a passing interest in military history, you might say." Not to mention it was part of the job to research the places he traveled to. "Now, the passenger?"

Josh opened the door to reveal a middle-aged gentleman dressed in a rumpled suit, wearing a perturbed expression.

Shaun sat at Parsons's desk across from the passenger. "Roger Howard? Thanks for meeting with us. I assure you that, despite the hour, it's for good reason."

Roger folded his hands on the desk and scowled. "I don't appreciate being woken at five in the morning and dragged to the security office like a common criminal."

He'd appreciate it even less if he was the one who'd been hurting Lexie. "From what I hear, there was no literal dragging involved, so let's stay focused. At least you've had some sleep, Mr. Howard, and I didn't ask you here without cause. Mind telling me what you were doing on a restricted deck around seven last night?"

Roger grunted and leaned back in his chair, straightening his tie. "I'm afraid I don't know what you're talking about."

"Think back, Mr. Howard. The engine deck is a passenger-restricted area."

"Sorry, I was in my cabin."

"What I think, Mr. Howard, is that you were skulking around to check on your smuggled cargo."

The man sat bolt upright, smug demeanor falling away. "Smuggled cargo? I did no such thing!"

"But you admit you were on a restricted deck."

Roger Howard clenched his jaw. He reached into his shirt pocket, pulled out a business card and slid it across the desk to Shaun.

"What's this?" Shaun picked it up, his stomach sinking as he read the card's writing: *Roger Howard, Federal Department of Maritime Occupational Health & Safety.*

"I'm a health and safety inspector." Roger tapped on the desk. "I conduct surprise inspections of Atlantic Voyages ships several times per year. This requires me to be on these restricted decks."

"And you didn't think to notify anyone?"

"Announcing my presence could compromise the inspection, giving time to hide or obscure the violations I'm hired to find. It's a matter of public safety."

Shaun resisted the urge to pound his head on the desk. A safety inspector? Of course. It made perfect sense. He dreaded breaking the news to Lexie. "If I call the number on this card, can someone at the department vouch for you?"

"Of course."

Shaun planned to follow up on that as soon as nine o'clock hit and the offices opened. "Mr. Howard, did you notice anything unusual during your inspection?"

Roger huffed and leaned back again. "Other than the door to the engine room being locked so I couldn't complete my rounds? No. I'll be trying again today, however."

Not likely. Shaun tucked the business card in his pocket and tried to hide his disappointment. He'd look into the man's claims, but Shaun believed him. The man's reactions seemed genuine, and his statements were easily verifiable.

Unfortunately, this made the lead a dead end. It felt like a weight in Shaun's gut. Two promising leads had come up cold in as many hours, which meant they were right back to square one.

Lexie woke with a crick in her neck and a stiff back. She'd fallen asleep on the couch by accident, having only intended to sit and take a load off for a few minutes. As comfortable as the plush couch was to sit on, it provided a terrible sleeping surface. She sat up and clasped her hands together, stretching in all directions. It didn't help. Everything still ached.

A clock on the far wall revealed another surprising truth, and Lexie blinked twice, wondering if her vision had suffered, too. No, there were the numbers, plain and clear. Just after four o'clock in the afternoon. No wonder she felt groggy and light-headed—she'd slept almost twelve hours! She needed food and hydration, stat.

As Lexie rubbed the remnants of sleep from her eyes and wondered if the captain's quarters had a snack basket, reality sank in. If she'd been left to sleep for twelve hours, the icebreaker hadn't yet arrived. The ship's passengers were now officially on day two of their sixteen-hour ferry trip, and likely getting more annoyed by the hour. It'd be helpful to have Shaun here to give her an update on the status of their investigation.

No, *his* investigation, she reminded herself. He'd made that quite clear last night, and she'd been far too tired to resist or argue the point. Well, now she'd had rest, and after some sustenance she'd be ready to get back into the game. Certainly the past twelve hours hadn't gone entirely without new developments. Maybe Shaun had snapped out of his cold spell, too. Keeping her out of things? Please.

She hadn't come this far and survived this many attacks only to be sidelined.

Lexie stood and stretched her legs, wishing not for the first time that she'd slept in her own room. What she wouldn't give for her bags and a shower. And her toothbrush. She debated leaving the captain's quarters, despite Shaun's plea for her to stay safely inside, but that yearning for cleanliness was satisfied when she realized her bags had been dropped off in the room while she slept.

Forty-five minutes later, Lexie felt mildly refreshed. The shower had helped soothe her aching muscles, though it'd done nothing for her famished insides. Hadn't Shaun promised to bring food?

Right on cue, the door handle jiggled. Beeps from the outer control pad suggested the visitor was a friendly—or so she hoped. She gave her towel-wrapped hair a final squeeze, unrolled and hung up the towel, grabbed her comb and headed back to the couch.

The door opened, and Shaun poked his head inside. "I heard the shower a little while ago. You're decent?"

The question made her smile. "I should hope so."

"Excellent." He sounded less angst-ridden than when they'd parted ways the night before, but Lexie couldn't say for sure if she was reading him right. He pushed the door open the rest of the way, revealing a tray laden with a veritable feast. Lexie's stomach rumbled at the scent of bacon, eggs and toast. A steaming mug of coffee and a glass of orange juice sat in either corner of the tray.

"I thought we were almost out of bacon." Lexie picked up a slice and inhaled the greasy but oh-so-appealing scent. "Not that I'm complaining."

"You wouldn't believe what can be accomplished with a little politeness." He pointed to the coffee. "One cream. Hope you're still impressed."

She was, and felt an odd twinge in her chest at the realization that he'd bothered to remember how she took her coffee. Did his thoughtfulness mean he'd come back to his senses?

Shaun lowered himself onto the other side of the couch, his back stiff. "All joking aside, Lexie, I want to apologize for acting brusque last night. You have to understand, I've been working to bring this operation to a close for the past three years." He leaned forward, placing his forearms on his knees. "But you've got an interest in this, too, and the last thing we need right now is to be distracted by each other. I'm afraid that I'm putting personal feelings before logical actions, and I don't want an emotional choice to put you in more danger than you're already in. You've been hurt several times already, and I can't let that happen again."

How noble of him. Lexie could respect that, in

a way—but at the same time, he'd said himself that she had an interest in this investigation. "I'm an adult, Shaun. I understand the risks. I wouldn't be here if I didn't choose to be. I took this case on personally through Lead Me Home because I care about Maria and her family, and I want to see them reunited again. I want to see her graduation photos, hear her mother gush about her daughter's achievements, see her sister's face light up when they're reunited. Something I never had."

Shaun frowned and sat upright. "You know Nikki's disappearance was not your fault, right?"

Lexie polished off the piece of bacon between her fingers, feeling the rush of blood to her cheeks as nerves took over. "Think about it, Shaun. All three of us were on that trip to Botswana eight years ago. If I hadn't convinced her to come, she never would have met you, setting the whole thing in motion. That trip was the first cog in the wheel. I started those gears turning by bringing her along. She didn't want to go. If she hadn't, she wouldn't have befriended you and been rejected when she wanted more, and then she wouldn't have gone on the rebound and ended up who knows where."

"People have choices, Lexie. Life is a series of choices. Somewhere along the way, your sister chose to act and react the way she did. Just like I did." Shaun scooted closer to her on the couch, resting his hand on her knee. The sympathy in his eyes hit her hard. His words weren't the empty platitudes she'd heard from most people—he'd been there, made poor choices and lived with the consequences. And chose to change, or so he'd told her, but at this point it was becoming harder and harder to doubt him. As far as she knew, Shaun had never lied to her, not once since the day they'd met in Africa. Nikki, on the other hand, had always struggled with the definition of "truth."

Who was she to believe?

She kept her gaze down, picking at the scrambled eggs with her fork, taking tiny bites. "Do you ever think about her? About what might have happened if you hadn't brushed her off?"

Shaun leaned forward, resting his elbows on his knees. "Honestly? No, I don't. I thought we'd keep up the friendship, but she made it clear that I wasn't to contact her or your family ever again, and I respected her wishes. Besides, it's not healthy to dwell in the past and always wonder 'what if.'"

Like I am now, she thought. What if she opened the gates and let in the flood of emotion that threatened to drown her after the events of the past day? What if she admitted that she and Shaun had an inexplicable chemistry or even said it aloud? She had a feeling that he just might reciprocate, and the prospect was terrifying. Could she really be falling for him? Could he really have fallen for her?

"You know I'm still looking for her," Lexie

mumbled, grabbing her cup of coffee and gripping it so tightly that her knuckles turned white. "I might find her someday. I won't give up."

Shaun nodded. "You don't strike me as the kind of person who gives up easily. If anyone gets that, it's me. If there's anything I can do to help, let me know."

Lexie's heart both sank and leaped. Obviously Shaun had serious connections, whether he admitted it or not. Harnessing those resources could provide the break she needed to reunite her family, and yet, his offer seemed hasty. Too eager. Lexie swallowed against a rush of disappointment. Had Shaun only offered to help because he regretted not pursuing her sister?

Shaun watched with a heavy heart as surprise, hope and disappointment played across Lexie's face. He hadn't wanted to give her false hope, but the offer was sincere. It was also somewhat selfish on Shaun's part, as it meant he'd have to talk to her after they resolved the case on the ferry. And if it also resulted in bringing a smile to her face, well, even better.

Unfortunately, if Lexie hadn't heard from Nikki in eight years, it was unlikely that there'd be any new contact in the days ahead. His hope was that the CIA had info on her in a database somewhere, especially if Lexie's theory held true and Nikki had been kidnapped. One trafficking ring was as bad as the next, and sadly, the Wolf was but one blemish in a despicable global industry. On the side of hope, however, stood the equally important knowledge that various agencies around the world had been shutting down kidnappers and their schemes for decades. If anyone had seen her, he'd be able to find out.

So, why had Lexie reacted to the offer as though she'd been stung?

"For a while," Lexie said, hugging her legs tight against her chest, "I thought she'd up and left because of the kind of person her heartbreak turned her into. That she left and purposefully avoided our attempts to search or contact her. I'm sure now that she simply never had a chance."

Shaun's gut seized at the pain in Lexie's voice. He touched her arm, trying hard to separate his head and his heart, but they were fast becoming entwined for the second time in under twenty-four hours. "I'm taking this man down, and I'm taking his entire operation down with him. Understand? I'm going to do everything I can to free as many people as possible. Today, we start with Maria. Tomorrow, or whenever we get off this ferry, I promise that I will personally use the intel we gather from the Wolf to change the lives of as many people in captivity as possible. We're going to make a difference one way or another. I know that's not the same as bringing Nikki back, but God has a plan. Even if we don't understand it in the present."

Lexie's eyebrows lifted at the mention of God's plan. "Sure He does," she scoffed, taking another sip of coffee. "I did note, however, that you said *we*. Does that mean you're letting me back on the case I came here to do in the first place?"

He had a feeling he'd regret this, but in their few hours apart, he'd missed her constant presence and quiet fortitude. She made him want to be a better agent. A better man. "I stand by my reasons for wanting to keep you safe, but you're right. You came here to do a job, and we're the best people to help each other in this situation. Plus, it's boring out there without you." He smiled and squeezed her elbow, and to his delight, she reached across and poked his hand.

"Too many men with opinions out there?"

Shaun grinned. "Plus, none of them are as cute as you."

Lexie laughed and tossed one of the couch's throw cushions at him. "Well, today's your day, Shaun Lane, because I refuse to take on any case without an attractive man by my side."

Shaun let his expression fall. "Guess this is where we say goodbye, then."

The tension between them momentarily evaporated as Lexie's genuine laughter broke down the remainder of the wall he'd erected the night before. Her smile was as lovely as he'd imagined it would be, but even lovelier was the woman behind the smile. She'd shown him her heart by revealing the truth of their past, and knowing that Nicola's disappearance drove her to help others avoid the same pain she felt tugged at his heart in a way he'd never known before.

He couldn't deny it—he was falling in love with Lexie Reilly.

As nice as Lexie found it to forget about the reason why they were sitting together in the captain's quarters, reality came rushing back in as soon as Shaun pulled out a folded sheet of paper from his pocket. The passenger list!

Shaun updated Lexie on his time spent speaking with the snooping passenger, which had turned out to be a dead end, and the work he'd done on the list while she slept. As Lexie polished off the last bite of toast, he suggested they head back to the computer room to finish combing through passenger details on the Atlantic Voyages database, a suggestion for which she felt genuinely grateful. The moment had turned too lighthearted, especially considering the situation. He seemed to understand that, and why wouldn't he? She had to remember that he'd been working this case for years, that this sort of situation wasn't new to him.

He cared, or else he wouldn't be working on it with such dedication. She could use a man like him at Lead Me Home, though she'd never be able to offer a comparable salary or benefits.

It made her grin just to think of making that offer. *Say, Shaun, I have this job opening...*

"What's so funny?" he asked as they trudged down the now-busy hallways toward the computer room. "I realize they're playing terrible '70s jams over the hall speakers, but I don't find it that hilarious."

He winked at her and she returned the gesture with a light whack to his shoulder, but the banter now seemed forced. The Wolf was still on board and still a serious threat—a man had been murdered just over twelve hours ago, only a few decks below them. And Maria remained missing.

It was a sobering thought. Lexie felt blood drain from her cheeks. Her feet froze in place. Anyone they passed could be the killer—anyone could reach out at any second, stabbing one of them in the neck—

"Lexie! Stay with me." Shaun turned around and gripped her forearms. "We're in public. You're safe. The Wolf doesn't want his organization exposed, so he's not going to try anything while there are so many people around. We have a few hours before the public spaces start to clear out for the evening, so let's use them wisely."

The Wolf might not be willing to try something, she thought, but he could be watching them right now. Observing everything they did and every move they made.

"Hey, Shaun?"

Shaun looked back at her and stopped, both of them stepping to the side of the hall.

"Are you sure the Wolf didn't know we were going to be in the library?"

Shaun shrugged. "I don't see how he could have. It smacks of a crime of opportunity. Remember, I went back to check later, but everything had been removed. Someone rigged it and then covered their tracks while security was distracted by evacuating us to the med center."

"I guess that makes sense. We haven't seen anything directly pointing to anyone, yet. This guy is a professional at covering his tracks."

Shaun rubbed a hand along his jawline, thinking. "All I can say is, we believe this guy has run his trafficking operation for at least a decade, so he's an expert at not getting caught. I don't claim to understand his psychology, but I do know he's no stranger to pulling off schemes that avoid detection."

Lexie nodded, though she still had a nagging feeling about how the whole thing had been pulled off. "And the engine room, that's bothering me, too."

Shaun leaned against the wall and crossed his arms. "Our killer had only a few minutes between us leaving and returning."

"He couldn't have been on the way down, done that and then left the room, correct?"

"Not in that time span."

"What if...what if the Wolf didn't actually leave the engine deck? If he didn't have time to do all that before we got there, maybe he never left."

"Or maybe he was in the room with us."

Lexie took a deep breath, remembering when they'd rounded the upstairs corner to find Josh waiting with a stun gun. He'd been right outside the elevator doors, without the other men on the team. Could *he* have ridden the elevator back up and waited outside of it until they arrived? But Josh didn't have any blood on his clothes, and he wouldn't have had the time to change and wash up before beating them to the elevator. The timeline wasn't physically possible. And Parsons had saved them from the gas attack in the library, which ruled him out.

"I'm starting to wonder if we've been looking in the wrong place this whole time," Shaun said.

"You think someone's lying to us?"

"I think it's a possibility. I know that Mr. Howard, the health and safety inspector, is legit. I looked him up and called his office. We might want to start considering a wider net, like the captain. Or someone running admin at the harbor on the island." Shaun reached for her hand and she instinctively flinched. They might have talked out their problems, rather, her problem with him, but it would take more than a few minutes of conversation to make it all better. She'd held on to those memories of Nikki too tightly for too long to erase her subconscious perception of the man in front of her just like that. No matter how sweet he'd been thus far.

They continued their journey in silence, Shaun leading the way to the computer room. Upon reaching the room, they discovered that the terminals were all occupied by families and passengers in the midst of frantic emailing—no doubt trying to salvage travel plans or make arrangements for pets or loved ones at home.

"We're still not saved, huh?" Lexie glanced out the window at the fading sunlight. "I didn't realize how long it takes to break up ocean ice with a ship. You sure you can't use your spy creds to get one of those computers for us?"

"Spy creds?" Shaun chuckled. "You really don't know how this works, do you?"

Lexie shrugged. "Just what the movies tell me. Spies get away with everything, it seems."

"Welcome to the real world, Miss Reilly. Spies are people trying to do their jobs. And for the record, I do have a small computer in my room that

I can hook up if I need to, but I thought you'd feel safer in a public space."

They left the computer room and headed down two decks to Shaun's cabin. As Shaun unlocked the door, an alarm sounded on his walkie-talkie, the red light on top flashing to indicate an incoming call. He paused to wait for the message, but nothing came through. "That's weird," he said, frowning at the device. "Must have been an accidental button press."

"Can you pocket dial a walkie-talkie?" Lexie asked, amusement in her voice.

"That's one benefit of old technology," he replied, tapping the device. "No accidental pocket photos, either." He pushed open the door to his room, quickly scanning to ensure no one had beaten them there. Considering that the Wolf always seemed to know where they were, a little extra caution was warranted.

Lexie remained in the doorway, standing with her hands in her pockets. He noted that she'd chosen a flattering red T-shirt and comfortable-looking brown corduroy pants after her shower, making him feel like a grubby hobo in his day-two plaid shirt and heavy jeans.

She tucked a strand of hair behind her ear. "Are we taking your computer back to a public area?"

"Captain's quarters," he said, hoisting a small bag over his shoulder. "It's the most secure room on the ship. I'll store it there when we're done with it, in case we need it again. Easier access that way."

The alarm sounded on the walkie-talkie again, beeping twice. Shaun pulled it from his belt and pressed the call button to open the channel and reply, despite hearing nothing from the other end. "Parsons? That you?"

Several tense seconds passed, terrible scenarios playing instantly through Lexie's mind. Had something happened to the security team while Shaun had come to check up on her? If she'd been the cause of more trauma, she'd never forgive herself.

The alarm sounded for a fourth time. Seconds later, a faint voice crackled through the static, cutting in and out. "H—o? Is any-n—ere?"

Lexie's insides seized. The voice sounded female. And scared.

"Who is this?" Shaun glanced at Lexie, worry clear on his face.

Seconds ticked by like hours before the next message came through. "We're tra—d. We're—boat. Please help."

Lexie's pulse sped up at the request for help. "Shaun?" Her voice was barely a whisper. She felt as if the world might evaporate around her if she spoke any louder, and a ringing grew in her ears. "Ask…ask her name."

Shaun nodded, fiddling with the dials to try

and clear up the static. "You're safe to speak. I'm Shaun, and my friend Lexie is here with me. Can you tell me your name?"

Static crackled through the speaker. Lexie held her breath, wishing she could jump through the radio to find the caller. The caller whom she knew, without a doubt, had to be—

"My name is Maria."

THIRTEEN

As Maria identified herself, Shaun had to remind himself to keep breathing. If that was truly Maria on the other end of the line, the game had changed once again. On the other hand, if Maria had been coerced into contacting Shaun and Lexie as part of the Wolf's twisted plan to trap them all and get them out of the way, they needed to move with even greater caution.

A tiny intake of breath to his right caused Shaun to refocus on the woman in front of him. Lexie's face had drained of color, and she swayed on her feet. He reached out a hand to steady her, helping her remain centered and stable as they worked through this critical moment. To his surprise, Lexie leaned in to his touch. He placed his arm around her shoulder, feeling her tension release. As much as he wanted to pause the moment and savor the breakthrough, the next few seconds could mean the difference between bringing Maria home and losing track of her forever.

"Maria," Shaun said, racking his brain for the right words. "We're very glad to hear from you. I understand you're not sure where you are, but there are many people searching for you. Anything you can tell us is helpful. Look around. Can you describe what you see?"

"Nothing, really," Maria said, voice quivering and uncertain. "We were in a room with a loud rumble until a few hours ago. Sounded like some kind of engine."

"You didn't see it?" Lexie focused on the space in front of her feet. "How'd they get you on board?"

"It's a long story, but this guy gave us something to drink. He said it'd be good for seasickness. I didn't want to drink it, but... Lexie, are my parents okay?"

"Drugged," Shaun whispered away from the walkie-talkie. "Like your coffee."

"Your parents are worried," Lexie answered, nodding at Shaun. "But it's going to be all right. I'll find you."

"You said they moved you?" Shaun closed his eyes and tried to imagine the scenario. If Maria had been in the engine room, no wonder he and Lexie had been attacked there during their search. And since there was the possibility that Shaun would go back and try to figure out what had happened, Maria had probably been moved to another isolated area.

"The guy who comes in, he wears a ski mask and brings us water that he watches us drink. We kept falling asleep, but the last time we woke up, it was a different guy. Shorter. And we'd been moved to another room."

Shaun glanced at Lexie, checking to see if she'd noticed Maria's constant use of the plural. Lexie's mouth hung open, her breaths deepening to control the rising anxiety of the moment. Yes, they'd definitely heard that right. "Maria, did you say *we*? Who's there with you?"

Maria's voice returned after a pause. "Dana and Jamie. Jamie…they shot her in the thigh when she tried to scream for help. We cleaned the wound with water and the guy who did it promised to bring some painkillers, but it's been hours and I think she's getting a fever. I'm worried it might be infected."

Three girls. Three. Maria's revelation changed everything. Shaun could no longer make this mission about taking down the Wolf. This news turned his focus into a full-scale retrieval op. Maria had been Lexie's initiative, but with the futures of three young women on the line, he needed to change his focus to match Lexie's—something he probably should have done from the very beginning. He'd been selfishly focused on how badly

ing up at him. "I…I knew, you know? But it wasn't real enough until now. I mean, it's one thing to have somebody try to kill *me*, but these girls… You know what Maria's mother said to me when she came to Lead Me Home for help?" Shaun remained silent, allowing Lexie to speak her mind without interruption. "She said, 'bring my daughter home, but if you don't—if you can't—I trust God's providence. I won't blame you.' Shaun, what does that even mean? How could she possibly be okay with that? I can barely breathe, hearing Maria's voice. If we don't find them, I don't know how I'll live with myself."

He took her hand and squeezed, wanting nothing more than to pull her into his arms and make all of her sadness and pain disappear. "I get it. I do."

He was all too familiar with the bewilderment that came alongside realizing the truth of just how cruel humans could be to each other. Lexie's compassion ran deep, deeper than she even knew. He saw it, though…because someone else had seen it in him on the day a little girl—no more than six or seven—had gripped him around the knees and cried with gratefulness that someone had finally come to save her.

He'd been in Thailand with a team on a drug bust. What they'd found there instead, hidden in a dank room with little water and no food…

Well, he'd never forget the eyes of that little girl, full of hope in a hopeless moment. That moment changed his life. He hadn't even known he could care so deeply for someone, or something, until then. Lexie was realizing it now, and it would hurt.

"I know you don't feel like rushing around, but we have to move." Shaun gripped both her hands and helped her to her feet. "We don't have much time. Never do, it seems."

Lexie drew her hands from his, pulled a hair tie from her wrist, and twisted her chestnut locks into a messy bun. "I know. Maria put them in grave danger by stealing a walkie-talkie and calling us. Isn't the Wolf, or whoever, going to notice? And know she called us? If he always knows where we are... Shaun, what if he's been listening in, too?"

He'd considered that time and again. Anyone who'd brought their own walkie-talkie on board could feasibly listen in if they found the right channel. "It's going to be okay. I know I shouldn't promise things I can't control, but I promise you this—I'm going to do everything in my power to keep you and those girls safe."

The silence that followed made him doubt whether she'd heard him at all. Finally, she leaned back against the wall and folded her arms. "I know you will, Shaun, but you're right." Her sharp gaze pierced through him, and he sat a little straighter at the tone of her voice. "You shouldn't promise what you can't control. After all, you can't deny they're after you, too—and if you keep looking out for me, who's going to keep *you* safe?"

Lexie felt numb, inside and out. The past fifteen minutes had passed like a hazy dream, morphing from hopeful exuberance to nightmarish despair and back again. Maria's father had been spot on when he'd described his daughter as feisty. Lexie only hoped that Maria's feistiness didn't get the girl and the other two with her killed.

Lexie wanted to accept the call as genuine, but Shaun's ongoing skepticism had begun to creep into her psyche. Combined with the worry over the dead air at the end of Maria's call, Lexie didn't know whether to hide herself in the nearest closet or race around opening doors until she found the girls. At the very least, her gratefulness for the anonymous tipster to Lead Me Home had increased—the only regret being that she couldn't thank him or her in person.

Shaun led the way from his room toward the security office, flying through empty stretches of hallway and sauntering by groups of passengers to minimize alarm. When they reached the office hallway, Shaun broke into a sprint as Lexie followed behind.

"Parsons!" Shaun shouted, yanking Lexie from her speculations. "We've got to move!" He came to an abrupt stop before the office door, causing Lexie to run into his back with a light thud.

Parsons's head poked out the door. Seeing them, he stepped out and locked the office in one deft motion. "You're in a mighty hurry," he mused, reattaching his keys to a belt loop. "Aren't you supposed to be trekking through the rest of the passenger list?"

"We got a call from the girl," Shaun said, waving his radio and sliding his computer bag from his shoulder. "I'll just be a sec, I need to drop this in the captain's room. I should have left it in my room, but I got distracted by the call. We may need to use it later anyway."

"No need." Parsons reached over and snatched the bag out of Shaun's hand. He plopped it inside the office and shut the door. "You can leave it here."

Shaun frowned, glanced at Lexie and gestured at Parsons to return the bag. "No, thanks. I have my own reasons for wanting it in the other room."

Lexie raised her eyebrows, but caught on to his subtle hint to back him up. "That way I can use it if I need to, and I won't have to bug your team to unlock the office."

A tic pulled the corner of Parsons's mouth toward the floor. A half second later, his expression cleared and he reopened the office, pulling the computer bag back out. "I can drop it off in there if you'd like. I'm headed that way now."

"Thanks, but I've got it." Shaun's tone had turned flat. He took the computer from the security officer, who seemed reluctant to let it go. The two men looked at each other in silence for a moment until Parsons cleared his throat, glancing over Shaun's shoulder at Lexie.

She started, surprised by the acknowledgment. It was the first time the man had bothered to make direct eye contact with her the entire trip. Something about his look made her shift uncomfortably, and she folded her arms across her stomach.

Parsons's attention wandered off of her as quickly as it had landed. "You said a call came through on the radio? From the missing girl? Need me to call the others?"

"Please," Shaun said, his tone shifting again as though the past thirty seconds hadn't happened. What had that been all about? Did the man resent Shaun's aptitude at the job Parsons should really be doing? Josh and Reed rounded the corner just as Parsons pulled his walkie-talkie off his belt. "Here they are. Guys, we have a major development."

As Shaun gave the security team a bare-bones rundown of Maria's call—leaving out, Lexie noted, any specifics of where she might be located—Lexie's attention wandered. She preferred not to relive the moment the call cut out, dwelling instead on—

On the belts of the two younger security officers.

Reed's walkie-talkie was clipped in place as expected, but Josh...Josh's radio was missing. Could he really be that careless not to notice its absence? And then she noticed that he'd noticed her watching him. *Oops.*

Josh's gaze hardened and Lexie swallowed the desire to let the moment pass without a word. If she didn't say something first, she'd be giving him the upper hand. "What happened to your walkie-talkie?"

Parsons and Shaun stopped talking. Silence fell over the group as surprise registered on Josh's face. He looked down at his belt and then at the staring faces around him. "It's charging in the staff room. I ran out of juice about forty minutes ago. Reed here can attest to that."

Reed tapped his own walkie-talkie. "Tried to call him a little while ago, but no answer. We bumped into each other on the way back up."

Shaun coughed. "Back *up*?"

Reed shrugged as Josh scowled and replied, "Figure of speech."

"But you didn't see him put it on the charger?" Lexie heard the tremble in her voice, but hoped the others would mistake it for exhaustion. "Can we go get it? We should all have a way to communicate with each other."

"I have a spare," Parsons said. "I can get it from the office here."

"No, I'd rather we go get the other one," Lexie said. "It wouldn't do to leave radios lying around."

The typically quiet Reed laughed. "We do it all the time in the staff areas. It's not a big deal." He whacked Josh in the arm. "Get one from here."

"Sure," Josh said with a shrug. "I was going to pick it up in about twenty minutes, but whatever."

Lexie snuck a questioning glance at Shaun, whose attention snapped between Josh and Parsons. If only she hadn't allowed her emotions to take over after Maria's call. She should have formulated a plan of approach with Shaun instead of heading in blind and leaving him to do the talking. She didn't usually operate that way—trusting someone else to take the reins—but Shaun had the kind of strength and confidence to make her comfortable enough to trust his judgment. Did that mean she should extend that trust to other things… like the events of the past?

"We need to get searching," Shaun said, casting a glance back at Lexie. She caught the meaning behind the look—he'd developed his own suspicions, but now wasn't the right time to address them. Not yet. "We'll take the lower passenger decks, you guys take the top two. Sound good?"

"I'll go with you two," Josh said, crossing the distance to stand by Lexie. "Then we'll have enough muscle on each team in case we run into trouble." The man patted his empty radio case and snuck a look at Parsons.

With a grunt, Parsons unlocked his office again and disappeared inside, closing the door behind him. He emerged with another walkie-talkie and shoved it into Josh's outstretched fingers. "Keep track of this one or it's coming out of your paycheck."

"Told you, I didn't lose it."

"You know what I mean."

Lexie's intuition nudged her, suggesting that Josh's company might not be the best idea. "He can't come with us," she said, soft enough for only Shaun to hear.

Shaun's nod of agreement was almost imperceptible. "It doesn't make sense to have a team of three and a team of two," he addressed the waiting men. "Our strategic advantage will come from the element of moving quickly and with surprise. I recommend teams of two, plus one person back here on middeck to respond immediately as backup for either team as needed. If we need further backup, whoever is farthest from the incident location can retrieve medical or other staff."

"I really think—" Josh began.

"The man's right," Parsons interrupted, glaring

at his team. "You and I will go together. Reed stays back—you're light on your feet, son."

Lexie took careful note of the color draining from Josh's cheeks. Should they have paid closer attention to the man's whereabouts during the trip? If he was the one they were looking for—be it the Wolf or another accomplice, despite the impossibility his role in several of the scenarios—would he make a move against Parsons? The burly head of security sure looked as if he could take on Josh, but the way Parsons continued to glare at his officer, it appeared he might take out the man first for showing up without his radio.

"Sounds good." Shaun interrupted Josh's protests. "Stay in contact. Keep the channel open at all times, and check the ones around it, too, in case the girl tries to contact us again."

Shaun placed his hand on Lexie's back and ushered her away from the three security men. She felt an urge to look back at them and see what transpired as when they left, but Shaun grunted beside her. "Don't. Let it play out."

"But what if—"

"Trust me." He guided them toward the nearest set of stairs. "If my suspicions are correct, we'll find the girls and be long gone before they've dealt with whatever's going on there."

FOURTEEN

Lexie winced at the noise they made trampling down the metal staircase. Though she couldn't fathom what Shaun had planned, she felt confident in his judgment. Quite the change from a little over twenty-four hours ago, when all she'd seen in him had been a wannabe hero with a penchant for getting himself into trouble.

How had this man worked his way into her heart in such a short period of time? Shaun's offer to check his sources for information about Nikki had been the kicker—she couldn't deny that the offer went above and beyond any involvement she'd expected him to have in her life. After all, when they found the girls and finally made harbor, she'd head back to small-town Ontario and he'd go back to Langley...or maybe he'd head overseas for a new mission.

Regardless of where he went, she couldn't follow. And why would he want her to? Allowing herself to feel anything beyond trust in the immediate situation simply didn't make sense. They had no possible future together. Certainly Shaun had to realize that, despite his flirtatious nature. She'd already seen that more than once, and hadn't done much to discourage it. Maybe that was her mistake.

Yet he'd also been nothing but a perfect gentleman. Had she read him wrong? Maybe she'd become delusional out of fear, or maybe her subconscious was attempting to connect dots that weren't there. Still, his earnestness drew her like a moth to flame...so how long until she got burned?

The air suddenly felt thick and electric. She couldn't shake the memory of Shaun on the parking deck when they'd met again for the first time. His tender touch on her injured palm had said more than words ever could, and the very fact that he'd remembered how she liked her coffee—twice!—made her throat tighten with an unbidden sense of longing.

"Lexie?" Shaun pivoted on the staircase, eyeing her with curiosity. "You realize you've stopped moving, right? Is something wrong?"

Heat flooded Lexie's cheeks as a whole migration's worth of butterflies exploded in her stomach. *Get a grip, girl. Now is not the time, and maybe not ever. He's so wrong for you, and you know it.*

She said nothing, not trusting herself to speak

in the moment. She clanged down the stairs ahead of him, putting him out of her field of vision, and pushed open the door to passenger deck two in silence. But of course, Shaun stepped in front of her, checking both ways down the hall. She'd forgotten about that part of their agreement. Why did he have to stand so *close*?

An elderly couple exited their room about twenty feet down the hall, waving at Shaun and Lexie in greeting.

"Maritimers," Lexie commented, grateful for a neutral topic to focus on. "Must be locals. They're too calm and casually dressed to be tourists. That's a fisherman's hat he's wearing."

Her observation brought a tiny curve to Shaun's lips. "You'd make a good superspy yourself, Miss Reilly."

She warmed at the compliment, though warmth was the very thing she'd been trying to avoid. Maybe she should take a break from the search, step outside. Away from him. Permanently.

"Follow me and stay close," Shaun said, oblivious to her internal struggle. He tilted his head to listen to the sounds around them, then pulled the walkie-talkie off his belt and handed it to Lexie. "If anything happens, I want you to run. Find a safe place and call for help. Understand?"

"I can handle it," she snapped, feeling quite overwhelmed. Couldn't he just…leave her alone for a little while? Her guilt spiked at the confusion on his face. He didn't deserve to be snapped at because she had feelings for him. How middle school of her. "You're right. We're in this together. I'll get help, but I'm not going to leave you behind."

Shaun frowned and focused on her with the ferocity of a lion. "I'm not going to let you get hurt again, Lexie. You've been through enough already, and the next time we're attacked, I may not be so fortunate." He tapped where the bullet had grazed his shoulder the night before. "We're dealing with someone incredibly dangerous, and we may be walking into a trap. It's taken me three years to get this close, and I can't have the repercussions fall on you."

Lexie swallowed, her throat growing dry. Why hadn't he moved out of the way? "I know what I'm getting into. I'm just as much a part of this as you are now. Plus, you need me—you said as much when you brought my breakfast."

His expression grew thoughtful, the intensity calming to that of a mild summer storm. "I did, didn't I?"

Lexie's breath quickened as Shaun leaned closer, every ounce of his intent directed at her being. Why hadn't she moved out of the way? Why weren't her feet working? Her brain screamed at her to get away, to stop this nonsense while she still could, but her heart pushed her closer and closer to the scruffy agent she'd become so attached to in only a matter of a few short hours.

His strong hands gripped her shoulders and pulled her closer. She didn't resist as they were drawn together like magnets. Time stood still as his head descended to hers with a cautious optimism. Their lips brushed, a tender and soft gesture as he tested her willingness. When she didn't resist, his mouth lingered over hers, building Lexie's anticipation for the inevitable connection.

Just as she felt herself relax into the moment, he suddenly pulled back, frowned and walked away.

Stupid, stupid, stupid. Shaun's head buzzed with the frustration of letting himself get too deep, too quickly. They both had a job to do, and this would help neither of them.

But then, hadn't he been thinking about what it would be like to kiss her since the moment he'd realized that they were actually perfect for each other? Perfect in every way except timing. Another time, maybe…except that when this was all said and done, he'd be on another assignment and she'd be back to her job in Ontario. They didn't even live in the same country. How could he lead either of their hearts astray when a future together was an impossibility?

Despite all the opposition she'd given him since that first moment on the parking deck, Shaun had no doubt that they had almost shared a kiss that would have been incredible. Enthralling. Consuming. And totally, utterly distracting to both of them at a time when distraction meant the kind of failure they couldn't afford.

Still, he'd be a fool to assume he didn't have a very angry, hurt woman following several feet behind him. They trekked in silence, but the tension in the air had grown thick and stifling. He'd try to explain himself later—she deserved an apology—but right now he needed to focus on the mission.

The passenger deck they'd entered sounded much quieter than the upper decks, save for being closer to the noises made by the ferry's inner workings. Almost too quiet. Too empty. The hair on the back of his neck stood up as he sensed Lexie draw close behind him.

"I think I heard something," she murmured. Shaun grimaced but didn't turn around. He hadn't heard anything, and they'd been walking together this whole time. Then again, he'd also gotten lost in his thoughts, going a little deeper than acceptable for the present situation.

"Stop for a second, please," she said, louder this time. He did, acknowledging her request with a nod over his shoulder. Dismissing her hunch at this late stage in their search would be folly, especially when they'd been working together so well—*working* being the key word, here—but he had his doubts on this one.

"I don't hear anything," he replied, after a few moments of silence.

Lexie pursed her lips and backed up a few paces. "I heard it here, a little closer to the bank of elevators on this deck." She kept walking backward, eyes closed and hands cupped around her ears to focus sound. She stopped just in front of the elevator doors. "Here. It sounds like...beeping? Like an alarm clock."

A chill swept through Shaun and he bounded across the short distance to where Lexie stood. He copied her, closing his eyes and using cupped hands to locate the sound she'd heard. In an instant, the chill turned into a full tidal wave of cold terror.

The soft beeping she'd heard had changed from an occasional blip to a full-on constant buzzing. The closest passenger rooms were twenty feet away in either direction.

The noise came from inside the elevator.

Shaun grabbed Lexie's forearm and pulled her toward him. "Run!"

Lexie's bewilderment lasted only long enough for her to find her footing. Shaun sprinted down the hallway, half dragging Lexie behind him as the elevators exploded with a deafening boom.

The floor underneath them shook and they tumbled to the ground, Shaun summoning his strength to pull Lexie alongside him and encircle her in his arms. He winced at the impact of his knees against the floor. Shaun covered Lexie's head and neck, holding her tightly against his chest as paint, plaster and metal debris rained down around them. He prayed that no dislodged live wires would land on or near them.

The world went from the loud noise of devastation to the muted thrum of temporarily damaged hearing—they'd been too close to the blast to avoid it, and it would take some time for their hearing to return. The scent of burned plastic and sharp chemicals filled Shaun's nostrils, reminding him of the missing cleaning supplies.

Shaun gritted his teeth at the realization. Why hadn't he considered a homemade bomb a possibility and put all the supplies on lockdown after the gassing incident?

Breathing through his nose, Shaun squinted into the haze of the hallway. Dust floated in the air, obscuring his vision. The hall lights made several valiant attempts to revive themselves, but after a shower of sparks flew from the damaged elevator shaft, the lights and power failed with an anticlimactic flicker. If his hearing hadn't been muffled, Shaun imagined he'd have heard the buzz of failing electricity, followed by the thud and click of emergency power generators kicking in.

Seeing it was safe enough to unfurl themselves from their place on the floor, Shaun loosened his grip on Lexie. She lay still in his arms.

Shaun's heart squeezed as though placed in a vice. *Please, God. Don't take her from me. Not like this.*

Emotion took over as he struggled to recall the Agency's bomb protocol training. He drew blank after blank, all logical thought replaced by fear that the motionless woman next to him might stay that way. Why had he let his last hour with her be one of rejection and anger?

"Lexie," he whispered, taking her head in his hands. "Can you hear me? Please wake up."

He pulled her back into the safety of his arms and kissed her forehead as a ringing in his ears grew louder. Faint screams sounded in the distance. Other passengers? He should call for medical assistance. And security, too, to let them know where he and Lexie were, that they'd survived the blast. Why hadn't anyone tried to call him yet? Surely they'd heard the bomb go off and were no doubt evacuating the remaining passengers from these lower decks as quickly as possible.

Coming to his senses, Shaun reached for his walkie-talkie, but it was no longer on his belt. Had it fallen off when he hit the floor? He scanned the area around them, hope sinking as he spotted pieces of the device scattered across the floor, about five feet away. From where he lay, the damage appeared mostly superficial, but he couldn't be sure until he had it in his hands again. If the main components inside hadn't been too badly damaged—

Beside him, Lexie moaned. Shaun's heart tightened again. "Lexie? Talk to me. Can you hear me?"

She pressed a palm to her forehead and coughed, eyes squeezed shut. "Barely. You sound like you're shouting at me from a mile away. What happened?"

"Someone set off a bomb in the elevator." And they'd done an excellent job of it, too. The more he contemplated the sequence of events that had to have happened to place them in this position, the angrier he grew. "Perfectly timed, down to the wire."

Lexie peered up at him. "In the elevator?" She paused, realization dawning. "Oh, of course. The beeping. Apparently, I need to watch more spy movies. How naive of me."

"Not naive at all. Think about it. What kind of person sets off a bomb on a boat?"

"Are we going to sink?" Stark terror crept into her voice, and Shaun clasped her a little tighter. He loosened his grip when she coughed, hoping she didn't see the redness creeping into his cheeks.

The ship creaked and groaned around them.

Footsteps pounded on the deck above, but no one had yet ventured into the blast hall. The blast damage appeared to have been contained to around fifteen feet or so on either side of the elevators.

"I don't think so," he finally said, hoping his voice sounded steady enough to be reassuring. "I think this was localized. Specific to this hallway, I mean."

Lexie groaned and rolled away from him, both hands on her temple. "To this hall? But that doesn't make sense. Why set off a bomb down here, where there's barely anyone around? And next to the elevator? The only people around are—"

"You and me." Shaun pushed himself up onto his elbows, wincing at the sharp jabs of pain throughout every part of his body. Yesterday's bullet graze on his shoulder burned with the agony of a reopened wound. "We were the only people around at the time of the blast."

"That doesn't make sense. How could the bomber know?"

"That's exactly what I'd like to find out." Setting off a bomb inside an elevator with no one else around would require careful calibration and some very specific circumstances falling together perfectly. "It's a lot of trouble to go to, pulling off something like this. I agree it doesn't make sense."

"Why not just shoot us?" Lexie said, echoing his thoughts.

Downed electricity. Lack of civilian casualties. Limited blast radius. How had they been targeted? The whole thing spoke of careful, professional planning. He'd thought the Wolf would be feeling desperate and start making mistakes by now. Shaun had underestimated their opponent, and it had almost cost them their lives.

But we're still alive.

Shaun sat bolt upright, visually scanning the hall once again. "Can you stand?" he asked Lexie. She hadn't complained of any injuries, but she seemed like the kind of woman who'd break her leg and then try to shake it off as a sprain.

To his relief, she nodded as he helped her to her feet. "What's going on, Shaun? You look… frantic."

He was, and he wasn't in the mood to hide it this time. "I hate to say it, but we can't stick around here. Whoever set off that bomb is going to come looking for us to make sure they got the job done."

After the events of the past day and a half, Shaun knew one thing with absolute certainty—he did not want to meet the Wolf head-on in the middle of an exploded hallway.

They were sitting ducks so long as they stayed here. They'd be easily picked off with no witnesses or repercussions, which meant they were exactly where the Wolf wanted them.

FIFTEEN

Lexie shivered at the look on Shaun's face. His usually serene, contemplative expression had been replaced by one of untethered urgency.

"We have to move," he said, offering his shoulder to lean against as she tested her legs. Though she stood without pain, her whole body felt as though it had been hit by a freight train. Her back ached, but nothing appeared broken. "We don't have much time."

He picked up the smashed walkie-talkie and a handful of the outer casing's broken pieces, wearing his frustration clear on his face. Lexie wished she knew what to say, but last she'd checked, working at Lead Me Home hadn't offered the kind of physical and psychological training that accounted for potential bombings and repeated threats on her life. All told, it was a marvel she was still standing.

Shaun fiddled with the radio for a few moments to no avail. "It's too damaged," he grunted, tossing it back on the floor. More pieces of the device popped off and scattered as it hit the ground. "Let's move." He turned around to lead the way, but a reddish glow from the walkie-talkie's landing site drew Lexie's attention.

She grabbed for it, despite Shaun's pleas to leave it and get moving. The reddish throb came from inside the device, visible now that additional pieces of the outer casing had fallen off. Lexie pressed her index finger inside the radio and pushed a stray wire out of the way, revealing a tiny red LED that pulsed with a steady rhythm.

Lexie didn't have to be a trained spy to recognize *that* piece of equipment. She dug the rest of her fingers inside and pulled the LED and its sticky base out of the device. "Uh, Shaun?" She held it up and watched his eyes widen in the dim emergency lighting. "This is a remote GPS tracker, right? I think we've discovered how somebody knew when to set the bomb off."

Shaun crossed the space between them in a heartbeat, grabbed the component out of her hand and threw it on the floor. He stomped the heel of his boot down, smashing it into thousands of tiny pieces. "Not anymore," he muttered. "Try tracking us now."

As much as she appreciated his decisive action, a more disturbing prospect came to mind. "This is a security walkie-talkie, Shaun. We got it from those guys before the library gassing, right?"

Shaun nodded, placing a finger to his lips. He gestured for her to follow him, and they moved out of the ruined hallway in silence. Despite the heavy sounds coming from the deck above, Lexie didn't spot another soul as she and Shaun made their way through the halls of passenger cabins, listening at each door for any out of place sound.

Despite Shaun's reassurances that the destroyed GPS finally gave them the upper hand, Lexie looked over her shoulder every few minutes, unable to shake the feeling that they were being watched. Between Josh's missing walkie-talkie and the GPS tracker inside theirs, Josh had hit number one on their suspect list. Who knew the ship better than a person on the security team? It made sense to place trackers inside the walkie-talkies to keep tabs on all the team members. He could move around the ship with stealth and avoid detection that way, but it still didn't account for how he could have killed the engineer and cleaned up within the short time frame. Another accomplice? A few minutes on a computer would help narrow down or rule out the remaining names on the passenger list. For her part, she had a strange feeling about Reed, but Shaun hadn't mentioned the man, so she'd been trying to put it out of her mind—she couldn't draw the connection anyway, and Reed seemed a little too clueless to be in on a major scheme.

And as badly as it stung to think that someone so close to them might have played them all along, Lexie hadn't forgotten about Shaun's deliberate truncation of their almost-kiss. This hot and cold flip-flopping game they played needed to stop. It hurt too much to continue teasing her heart this way. The next quiet moment they had together, she'd give him an ultimatum: to make something of their undeniable connection, despite the difficulties, or to forget it altogether.

The latter sounded far easier. Less messy and complicated for her too-busy, no-time-for-a-relationship life. So why did such a large part of her heart hope he chose the former?

Lexie stopped abruptly, lost in her thoughts, when Shaun held up his hand and stopped in front of another cabin door. He pressed his ear against it, then motioned for her to do the same. Leaning in, Lexie's heart leaped into her throat when the faint crackle of static became audible through the door.

"Open channel," Shaun mouthed. He pointed at her and then at the floor. *Stay put.*

Lexie stepped behind him, just as she did when he'd checked her room for intruders that very first day. The door creaked open without resistance, causing Lexie's hopes to plummet. Someone hadn't bothered locking the door. Not a good sign.

No light filtered through the door crack, save for the harsh red-orange glare of an exit sign's ubiquitous lighting, and the only sound from within was that of a crackling walkie-talkie. Shaun crouched low and Lexie followed his lead. In a sudden burst of speed, Shaun aimed a low kick at the door, sending it flying open as he tucked and rolled into the room, coming up into a crouch with his gun in his hands.

Lexie froze in place seeing the weapon. Hadn't Shaun lost it in the engine room? He must have retrieved it since then, but the image of Shaun with a protective weapon in his hands made the danger of the situation all the more real.

He waved her into the room, and she pointed to her eyes and shrugged. *See anything?*

Shaun signaled thumbs-down as he swept the room. He checked the bathroom while Lexie peered under the bed, but the crackling noise of the walkie-talkie sounded loudest at the front of the room, near the closet. Shaun positioned himself to the side of the closet to have a full view and clear aim in case anyone waited inside for an ambush. Lexie fervently hoped that the only ambush would be from three frightened young women, eager to get back home to their families.

Lexie held up three fingers, tucking them away in a silent countdown. *Three...two...one...*

At zero, she yanked back the closet door and

ducked aside as Shaun aimed inside the storage area…and immediately dropped his arms.

"Empty," he said, ending the facade of silence. "Except for that." He reached inside and pulled out the walkie-talkie, its top light lit to show the channel had been left open.

"Someone beat us here." Lexie's heart sank. "They were here, though. I'm sure of it."

Shaun knelt and crawled inside the closet, patting down the space with his hands. He stood up with his palm open. A tiny object in the center sparkled in the room's poor lighting. "They made sure we knew it, too. Smart girls."

Lexie carefully plucked the small, silver earring stud from Shaun's hand. "From what Maria's sister tells me about her, this sounds like the kind of thing Maria would do. The girl has a bright future ahead of her." She swallowed, thinking about the kind of future Maria would have if they didn't find her. "Or at least, she should. She will."

"We'll make sure of it," Shaun said, tucking his gun back in his belt. "But we have to get out of here. Whoever tracked us through GPS knew we were coming down here, and they beat us to it. This walkie-talkie wasn't left behind by accident—" A thump from outside the room confirmed Shaun's words. "It's not easy to navigate out there with just those emergency lights. Let's move."

Shaun took Lexie by the hand, and they moved

as one to the exit. Just as Shaun reached the door, a black ski-masked figure appeared in the doorway. Lexie screamed as Shaun immediately drove his left elbow upward into the person's face. A muffled grunt was followed by a return swing, but Shaun followed through with a right hook that sent the attacker flying backward into the wall.

"Come on!" Shaun pushed Lexie in front of him and they took off down the hall in the opposite direction from where they'd come. A bang split the air and a sharp jab like a bee sting pricked Lexie's leg. She pushed it from her mind and kept moving as several more bangs followed. Behind her, Shaun grunted, but it sounded more like anger than pain.

"Are you hit?" she tried to call over her shoulder, but Shaun only gripped her upper arm and kept them moving. "Who was that?"

"I think," he said between exhales, breath coming fast and laborious, "that's our elusive friend the Wolf."

Lexie's heartbeat pounded triple time, and she sucked in gulps of stuffy air to try and quell the waves of nausea that threatened to overtake her. "How did he find us? You smashed the GPS."

Shaun grabbed her hand and pulled her around a corner. "He drew us right to that room. He knew we were coming. Probably checked the blast site first, didn't see bodies and—"

"Can't you just shoot him?"

Shaun chuckled, a humorless sound. "A fire-fight in this lighting is pointless. Notice that his shots are random? I'd rather save our rounds for a clear view. Right now, we run. Moving targets are much harder to hit."

Footsteps pounded toward the corner where they'd hidden. Shaun gripped Lexie's hand again and they were on the move, passing corridor after corridor, running blind in the dim lighting.

Lexie's lungs burned, her legs wobbling like rubber bands. The stinging sensation in her leg had increased to a full burn, and wetness tickled her skin as they ran. Was she leaving a trail for the Wolf to follow? She tried to look back, but the emergency lighting made it hard to see anything against the dark gray carpeting of the halls.

And then, like a lighthouse in the middle of an ocean storm, Lexie caught sight of a red-lit exit sign. By the time she realized what she'd seen, they were already past it.

"We need to go back," Lexie hissed, tugging on Shaun's shirt. "There's an exit. I think we can get to another deck from there. Maybe emergency stairs. But, Shaun, my left leg really hurts."

Despite the darkness, she couldn't mistake the look of incredulity on Shaun's face. "Wait, were you hit? He could be right behind us. How far back?"

"Maybe thirty feet? I'm hit but I can walk." She

desperately hoped she hadn't miscalculated. "And we haven't seen another exit yet."

With a nod, he turned around and squinted into the shadows. Then he tore off his right shoe, pulled off his sock and pushed up her pant leg. He tied the sock around her wound and put his shoe back on. "It's just a graze, but it's going to sting for a little while. The sock should absorb any more blood."

"Thank you." Lexie could no longer hear the footsteps that had dogged them—where *were* all the passengers?—but for some reason, that made it that much worse. She imagined their ski-masked pursuer waiting around a corner to jump out at them. "Can we make it to the exit?"

"I think we've lost him, but we may only have a few seconds. Go!" Shaun gave her arm a reassuring squeeze as fear flared in her gut. If she'd misjudged, they were done for. It was a marvel neither of them had been killed so far, considering all the bullets fired, but it appeared Shaun had been right in his statement that shooting in the dark was a waste of ammunition.

Lexie led the way back to the exit, certain that at any moment, shots would come firing out of the dark and it'd be over. The dim red glow of the word *Exit* felt like both a lifeline and a flashing neon sign saying "here we are!" She sprinted the last few feet to the door and placed both hands on the crash bar. Her surprise at its bitter coldness lasted only as long as it took to push the door open. A blast of frigid Atlantic winter air took her breath away in an instant, drying out her throat and nostrils.

Lexie's eyes swept from left to right as Shaun came through the door behind her, her heart sinking as goose bumps raised along her arms. They'd leaped out of the frying pan...and into the freezer?

The instant Shaun realized they'd stepped from the warmth of the indoor passenger deck to an outdoor winter wasteland, he tore off his puffy vest and threw it around Lexie's shoulders. The vest wouldn't keep out the cold for long, but it might stop Lexie from catching a chill while they determined their next move.

The outside deck sparkled in the moonlight, the result of a foggy day's condensation turned to freezing drizzle. The night's shift in temperature left a thin coating of ice on almost every surface across the deck—floor, railings, the nearby deck chairs. Shaun shivered, his plaid cotton shirt offering little barrier against the cold. He'd last longer than Lexie outside, but if they didn't figure out a plan soon, they'd have simply exchanged one deadly situation for another.

"Do you think he saw us?" Lexie asked, keeping her voice at a near-whisper. "If he didn't see us or hear us exit, maybe he'll search for a little while and give up. We can find a place to hide and outlast him."

Who'd outlast whom was what Shaun felt afraid of. "Or he's about to burst through these doors at any second."

He and Lexie were sitting ducks—neither they nor their attacker would be able to move quickly on the icy deck, and their attacker would have the simple advantage of remaining in the doorway to finish the deed.

"We should hide," Lexie reiterated, echoing his thoughts. "Are there storage sheds out here? For chairs or outdoor maintenance?"

A chill ran up Shaun's spine as he scanned the deck for a hiding space. It hadn't missed his attention that Lexie had already begun shivering, so any place they hid would need to be small and enclosed to preserve body heat. Otherwise, the Wolf wouldn't need to shoot them—he could just leave them out here to freeze, letting the weather do his dirty work for him.

"What about lifeboats?" Lexie took a tentative step in the direction of a lumpy orange tarp, about fifteen yards away at a section of deck with a gap in the railing. The rounded tarp appeared large enough to cover a lifeboat or two. On these types of ships, lifeboats were strung together high up, so that passengers could embark before being lowered down to the water.

"Good idea, except for one thing." Shaun pressed two fingers to the bridge of his nose. "As soon as we try to move the tarp, the ice on it will crack and leave shards across the deck. It'll give away our position."

"You sure about that?" Lexie broke free of the doorway, speeding across the icy deck like an expert skater, sliding one foot after the other on the slick surface. Moments later, she touched the orange tarp and waved at him with a slight grin. "Water repellant. It's one of the good ones."

Shaun couldn't resist a smirk as he joined her next to the lifeboats. "Camp *and* skate a lot, do you?"

"I used to," she said, her expression thoughtful. "I had an outdoorsy childhood. If we climb under here, we should be able to refasten the far corner from the inside. I don't see anywhere else to go."

"Let's do it. Mind the gap at the edge of the boat." Shaun helped her unhook the corner of the tarp and held it open as she crawled underneath. They'd spent far too much time figuring out what to do. Seconds made all the difference when it came to protecting oneself from the cold, and they'd already lost precious moments that could mean the difference between life and death. It didn't help that Lexie's mild shiver had become visibly more pronounced in the past thirty seconds.

With a final glance back at the door they'd

exited, Shaun's heart skipped a beat as he thought he heard the recognizable *thunk* of the crash bar smashing into place. He dove under the tarp, grateful that the ferry had secured their lifeboats firmly in place for boarding. The moment would have been made that much worse if their entrance to the lifeboat had caused it to swing back and forth.

Shaun reached two fingers underneath the tarp to reattach it to the boat's corner.

"I found a blanket," whispered Lexie as he settled into the spot next to her. "It's chilly, but it'll heat up in a few minutes."

Shaun didn't miss the chattering of her teeth as she tried to offer the blanket to him. He shook his head in silence. No way could he share that blanket with her. He'd been through training exercises designed to test his mettle in extreme temperatures, so he knew what his body could handle, but would Lexie recognize the signs of hypothermia if and when they set in? That blanket might be her lifeline.

A subtle click in the distance sent Shaun's senses on high alert. He shot a glance at Lexie, hoping she'd get the message. *We need to keep quiet, or this could end very quickly.*

Shaun drew his gun from his belt and slid onto his back, keeping the barrel raised for optimum range of motion in any direction. If the killer came anywhere close, Shaun would not hesitate to protect the woman next to him. He'd gladly suffer the consequences if it meant keeping her safe. She meant too much to him—he knew that now.

Another quick glance showed him that Lexie had her eyes closed tight. Was she praying? Lexie hadn't said anything about God, beyond seeming miffed when he'd suggested that his faith might play any kind of role in the work he did. Their discussion about the past hadn't come full circle to what she believed in the present. It was his fervent prayer that he'd get a chance to ask her about it once they were somewhere warm, safe and dry.

At the soft scrape of shoes sliding along ice, Lexie stiffened beside him. He yearned to reach out and comfort her, but deep inside he knew that she was stronger than he instinctively gave her credit for. She'd gone through so much since this whole ordeal began, and yet here she was, leading the charge to hide inside a lifeboat from a madman. Had Lexie possessed this kind of inner strength all those years ago, or had it been born of necessity? He hadn't bothered to get to know her back then—she hadn't been "fun enough" for him. But if he had to be trapped with someone right now, well, she'd stayed as level-headed as any fully trained agent, which only drew him to her that much more. He *needed* to bring them both out of here alive. He had so many questions to ask her, so many things he wanted to know...and so many wasted years to make up for.

Lexie's breathing softened and quieted. He looked over at her every thirty seconds to be sure she hadn't fallen asleep—because if he wasn't mistaken, the temperature outside kept dropping as the night grew deeper. After what seemed like hours, Shaun thought he heard the soft click of another door shutting, though he didn't want to look outside right away to check for sure. An intelligent adversary like the Wolf would know how to lure them out by creating a false sense of safety.

Shaun counted to one thousand before slowly and carefully unhooking the far corner of the tarp. He peered out at the empty deck, its surface shining like crystal under the clear winter sky. Under different circumstances, it would have been beautiful.

Shallow, ragged breathing startled Shaun into action. Lexie's eyes remained closed and she clutched the blanket to her chest, her entire body shaking violently. She'd go into hypothermic shock if he didn't find her a place to warm up soon. Staying outside at this point might prove a whole lot more fatal than a gunshot wound.

"Lexie?" He brushed his fingers against her forehead, though they were too cold and numb to feel much of anything. "We have to get inside. I need you to come out of the boat. Then I can carry you the rest of the way."

If she couldn't walk, he'd take her into his arms and carry her. It was that simple. But one way or another, they were getting out of this alive and together.

Her blinks were sluggish, chilling Shaun in a way that the frigid winter air couldn't. He needed to get her inside and warmed up immediately. Lexie propped herself up on one elbow with great effort. "Is it safe?"

"No one's out here, but we have to hustle. We need to get you inside as fast as possible. Bring the blanket, but wait here until I'm out of the boat so I can help you."

Shaun crawled out of the corner of the boat, which proved a more precarious task than getting inside of it. The deck's coating of ice made it difficult to find his footing, and he had to hook one foot on the inside of the boat and then use it to push himself away from the edge of the deck. While it hadn't posed a threat getting inside, the small gap between the end of the boat and the edge of the ship's deck was just wide enough to make him nervous. Under normal circumstances, it wouldn't be a problem, since lifeboats were lowered down once passengers stepped inside —people didn't typically get out of a lifeboat and back onto the main ship.

Lexie's head poked through the tarp as Shaun tried to find safe and secure footing to help her out of the boat. Before he could tell her to wait, she'd lurched upright in the lifeboat, blanket in hand, and taken a direct step onto the deck.

And then she slipped, with nowhere to go but four stories down onto solid ice.

SIXTEEN

Sheer terror flooded every vein as the earth slid out from underneath Lexie's feet. She flailed in the air, feeling her weight begin to free-fall. The blanket tangled around her arm, and though she tried to reach for the side of the lifeboat, her limbs refused to cooperate.

So...cold.

A vision of herself and Nikki, the day before her sister disappeared, flashed through her memory as she fell. Nikki's coy smile and teasing laugh, and Lexie feeling confused at her sister's exuberance...pity at her sister's need to find happiness in empty relationships. Jealousy at her sister's freedom? Yes, jealousy that her sister had a kind of personal freedom that Lexie never had. That she'd never felt she deserved, because she'd thought it was up to her to be the responsible sister, to take care of her ruined sister whose heart she'd believed had been broken by a selfish, heartless boy. Now she would never know that freedom for herself.

Her life would end on the ice below, broken and forever unfulfilled—

In the same instant, a strong hand grabbed the edge of the puffy vest Shaun had loaned her. The hand jerked her upward, gripped her wrist and pulled her forward. Lexie's legs slammed against the side of the ship with a bang.

"Stay with me," Shaun pleaded. "Look at me. Don't look down, keep your eyes on me."

Lexie pulled her gaze back up from where it focused, four stories down on the ice below. The lifeboat blanket slipped from her arm and drifted toward the ice, catching in the breeze. It made the descent look as peaceful as falling asleep.

"Up here!"

Lexie snapped out of it, realizing that the hand clasped around her wrist wouldn't hold for much longer—Shaun's fingers were beyond white, almost blue, and Lexie barely felt anything in her own fingers and toes. Shaun's other arm reached for her as he leaned over the edge of the ship. He had one leg braced against the lifeboat and the other precariously placed on the icy deck. He gripped under her shoulder and she grasped his forearm, following his directions to place her feet against the side of the ship and the lifeboat, straddle-walking her way back up.

A few tense seconds later, they were both back on the deck.

Lexie gulped down shallow breaths, panic threatening to overtake her senses, but the cold air burned her lungs and overrode the external triggers. Lexie didn't resist as Shaun bundled her into his arms and hustled across the deck, sliding one foot after the other. He took them through the first door, though the complete and utter lack of light barely registered in her consciousness as Shaun walked with purpose through the darkened halls.

"I'm sleepy," Lexie murmured, feeling the lull of exhaustion. She tried to cover her mouth as she yawned, but her arm refused to follow orders and she hit herself in the cheek instead. "Oops. Shaun, I think I need to lie down for a minute." What would a short nap hurt? They'd been running all day...all night...

A tingle began in her fingers and toes, rousing her from the sudden urge to sleep. By the time she felt herself being placed on the floor, the tingle had become a painful burn in all her limbs. At least it detracted her attention from the sting of her gunshot graze.

"Don't fall asleep," Shaun pleaded, grabbing her hands and placing them between his own. "Lexie, keep your eyes open. Talk to me."

Why should she talk to him? All she wanted was a warm bed, some coffee...wait, coffee... something about coffee...

The reminder of coffee jolted her brain back to

the present. "Shaun? Where are we? Are we safe?" The last clear memory she had was of diving into the lifeboat outside. "We have to hide."

Shaun searched her face, and half of her brain told her he sat too close. The other half wondered why the burning in her limbs wouldn't go away.

"I don't know if we're safe or not," he said. "We're going to wait in here a little while and try to warm up." He squeezed her hands between his, alternating between breathing hot air on their frozen fingers and rubbing the skin to increase circulation. Lexie faded in and out of consciousness as the tingling waxed and waned. Time's passage became irrelative to everything save the easing of pain from her numb extremities.

At some point, Shaun crossed the room and came back with a handful of candles, matches and a box of tissues. He must have seen the quizzical look she gave him, because he shrugged, pulled out a match and lit a candle. He placed it on the floor between them. "Take off your shoes and socks. I'll light a few more of these."

Lexie did as he asked, but the muddy candlelight made it even more difficult to tell where they were. "What kind of room is this?" Her words still sounded sluggish to her own ears. "How did you know this was here?"

"It's the ferry's prayer chapel. I saw it when we were making our rounds a while ago. There were a few candles lit in here earlier today, so I thought this might be our best source for fast heat. Looks like they've turned the power off on this deck, too, or at least in this section. The elevator explosion is one hall over and one floor below us, so they might have turned off the power to try and fix things. Might explain why we haven't heard any alarms or announcements yet."

Lexie nodded, gritting her teeth at the returning sensation in her fingers and toes. "Do you think they evacuated these decks?"

Shaun scooted across the floor next to her so they sat shoulder to shoulder. "I suspect that, since this floor is one floor above the explosion, it was evacuated while we were outside. We probably missed the ensuing panic right after the blast, which may be why our pursuer hasn't found us yet."

"Yet. That's reassuring." Lexie wished her fingers didn't hurt so much. He looked so discouraged, she actually thought she might hug him. Again.

Shaun rested his head against the wall. "Have to say, I'm feeling like a pretty unintelligent intelligence agent right now."

Lexie felt a grin spread across her face at his admission. "If it makes you feel any better, if I had to be stuck in the dark with anyone while on the run from an angry kidnapper, I'm glad it's with you. It means we have two brains working instead of trying to do this on our own." She hoped she hadn't said the wrong thing. Up until this moment, he hadn't shown any kind of self-doubt.

It was the right thing to say. He rolled his head against the wall to smile at her. "We do make a good team. I shouldn't be so negative. I trust that God's in control here, though sometimes it's hard to see His hand at work."

Lexie hardly believed the words coming out of his mouth. "The last I checked, the person in control of this situation is the person chasing us. But hopefully that changes soon."

"God provides, Lexie. He helped me catch you when you fell, and He'll help us get through this one way or another."

Despite her frigid limbs, heat flooded Lexie's cheeks as ire rose in her belly. Helped to catch her when she fell? So where did that put God when other people were in trouble? "What you're telling me is that God picks and chooses who to help. Like some kind of cruel game master."

Shaun blinked in alarm. "That's not what I'm saying at all. I'm saying I trust in His ultimate authority. God is the ultimate dispenser of justice. I'm hoping we take this guy down, but God's justice is what really matters in the end."

"That's a pretty raw deal for the people who get hurt in the meantime."

"We're not meant to understand everything, we're just meant to—"

"Sit back and watch as God takes away everything from us?" Lexie pulled her hands away from Shaun and tucked them under her armpits. She'd warm up her own way, thank you very much. "God doesn't care, and you can't tell me you actually think He does."

"He does."

"He *doesn't*." Lexie knew her voice had risen, but she couldn't stop it. He needed to know exactly why she didn't care for his garbage platitudes. Like cement hardening, the next phrase took shape before she could stop it. "If God cared? Nikki and I would have never met you. If you'd never been a part of our lives, never become friends with her, she wouldn't be missing today. So, *no*. I don't believe God cares."

A dark, harsh silence descended. The only sound in the candlelit blackness was Lexie's heartbeat. Could Shaun hear it? She didn't care. She didn't care if one more word ever came out of his mouth. As soon as they made it to shore, she'd leave Shaun whatever-his-last-name-was behind and never look back, not even once—

"I'm sorry, Lexie."

Lexie hardly believed her ears. "You're...what?"

"I'm sorry. I'm truly, honestly sorry."

Lexie stared at Shaun. His expression had

grown plaintive, the candles' white flame only accentuating the sadness and regret on his face. "Come again?"

"I'm sorry that I allowed your sister to be distracted on the trip. I was a selfish, narcissistic teenager, and even though she and I were just friends, I probably didn't help matters by goofing off most of the time. I came around eventually, but I guess it was too late to be a good influence on Nikki. Maybe I didn't explain myself when I let her down, maybe I could have been more compassionate. I don't know. If there's anything I did wrong, I'm sorry."

This was unexpected. Lexie's heart pounded harder as Shaun's gaze held hers with unshakable sincerity. "You can't be serious."

He reached over, gripping her hands in his once again. "I know I can't go back in time and make things better. None of us can, and it's not worth living our lives in regret. All we can do is our best in the present, living the way God wants us to live. Constantly striving to be more like Him as we move toward the future. After everything we saw on that trip, I wanted to try to be the best man I knew how, and I'm still trying to do that today."

All Lexie could do was blink. No other body parts seemed to be working. He was asking for her...forgiveness? Understanding?

When she didn't respond, he squeezed her hands

one more time and released them. "I realize you're angry, and you have every right to be. It's a lot to take in, and I don't have all the answers."

Her head, her logic, screamed at her not to forgive. Her brain spouted lies, telling her that he had ulterior motives, that he only said this because they were in the dark on the run from a killer. But her heart, when she looked into his eyes, knew the request came from a sincere man. A man of God who only wanted to do what was right.

After all this time, after all these years, she'd never imagined she would have a chance to give Shaun Carver a piece of her mind—or that he would ask her for forgiveness for an anger that she finally understood had nothing to do with him and everything to do with her sister's choices. He deserved no blame, despite being willing to take it for something that was never his fault. No, Lexie was angry with herself…angry for forcing her sister into a position where she'd taken a wrong turn, and for not being able to stop her or change her or bring her back from wherever she'd ended up.

Lexie inhaled slowly, counting the seconds as they passed. He waited for a response, and she needed to give him one.

But the words refused to come. She buckled, and the emotions she'd held back for so many years burst forth and spilled over. Shaun closed the gap between them, wrapping his strong arms around her once again. How could she respond to a request like that? After everything she'd done to him in anger—blaming him for years, projecting her anger onto him—he'd been the wrong person all along. He'd tried to do the right thing. Here was a man who knew about honor and trust, and she'd given him neither.

"It's not your fault," Shaun murmured into her hair, his breath warming her chilled exterior. "I know you think it's your fault because you made her go with you on the mission trip, but it's not. Your sister had free will, and so did I. So do you. God allows free will so that we can make our own choices. It's never been your fault, Lexie. You can't blame yourself."

"I'm sorry, Shaun," she whispered into his shoulder. "I've been so angry at you all these years, but I forgot the very lessons I'd gone on that mission trip to learn in the first place. I hope *you* can forgive *me*."

With a gentle laugh, Shaun smoothed his hand over her hair and kissed her forehead. "I already have."

"I can't give up on her." Lexie hiccupped through her sobs. "I know Maria isn't Nikki, but I can't give up on her—on knowing what happened to her. God did, but I can't."

Shaun placed his hands on her cheeks, linking

their gaze together like chains. "God never gave up on Nikki. Not once. And He's never given up on you, either."

It was a truth she knew from childhood, but how long had it been since she'd believed it? And yet, here was an undeniable case of redemption right in front of her. How could she have been so blind for so long? People changed, the same way she had. Only she hadn't changed for the better. She'd allowed herself to become bitter and angry, blaming herself for something she had no control over and never would.

Life was too short to stay angry, to hold grudges. To say "later" or "can't." Who knew what would happen once they made their way out of this mess, if they ever did? What mattered was that they were here together, right now, in this moment. He cared deeply for her, she knew that—and somewhere, past the fear and the physical pain of the injuries of the past thirty or so hours, she cared for him, too. More than she'd been willing to admit. Her heart had been chained by anger for too long. And now, after so many years, the burden of anger and guilt, as heavy as a mountain, lifted from her shoulders.

She knew with firm certainty that she'd held back long enough. She tilted her chin upward, parted her lips and waited. Gently, and so tenderly, he took the invitation.

* * *

Shaun filled the empty space between them, knowing that this time, he wouldn't pull away. This was no old memory. This was a new, here-and-now connection of two hearts that knew exactly what they wanted, despite the difficulties and danger.

Time had no meaning until the moment their lips parted, when an instant sense of loss enveloped Shaun.

Lexie drew a shaky breath. "We have terrible timing."

Shaun threw his head back and laughed. Lexie joined in seconds later, and they giggled their lost years away until finally stopping to catch their breath. They rested their foreheads together, a small moment of peace amidst the hours of non-stop, hectic stress and danger.

Minutes ticked by, and while Shaun wished that he and Lexie could enjoy their moment of tranquility for a little while longer, the reality was that a madman still lurked about in the corners of the ship, searching for them.

"Do you think it's safe?" Lexie pulled back, searching his face for answers. "How long should we stay here?"

"I was about to ask the same thing." Shaun tucked a loose strand of her chestnut hair behind her ear, his fingertips lingering on the soft skin behind her jaw. "We're not in the clear yet, but if we just keep going the way we're going, we'll never know for sure."

Lexie raised an eyebrow. "Are we still talking about the masked gunman?"

He shrugged. "You pick."

They cracked another smile together, but Shaun noticed that Lexie had begun to tremble again. She'd warmed up enough to be out of immediate danger, but both of them needed medical attention to check for frostbite. "I know you're going to try and shut me down on this, but we need to get you out of here right away. I'm going to make my way upstairs and bring the medical team here to retrieve you, okay?"

"Alone? No, I'm going with you."

"Not this time." He touched her feet and rubbed her toes. "Can you feel that?"

Lexie bit her lip. Clearly she didn't want to tell him the truth. It was worse than he'd thought. "I can, but not well. My toes are still burning, but they don't feel cold."

"I don't want to risk you walking. If you're injured, you'll only hurt yourself further—and on the off chance that the gunman is still searching these decks for us, you're not going to be able to run. That said, I don't think he's close, or else he would have heard us by now."

Lexie's mouth curved into a tiny smile. "Guess we haven't been all that quiet."

"Not exactly." Shaun rolled up into a crouch, checking his waistband to be sure that his gun was still tucked in place. "But if I'm out there moving around, I'll be guaranteed to draw his attention away from here. We'll move you to the corner of the room with the candles. You'll have some warmth, but the light shouldn't be visible from the doorway."

Shaun kissed the back of her hand and moved the candles to the farthest corner. He hated the idea of leaving her here alone, but she really would be safer. He'd also try to find out why the power hadn't been restored yet, and possibly get the lights turned on. Medical could bring a stretcher down and cart her off to someplace warm.

"What about you?" Lexie's nervous smile intensified with worry, and she peeked over her shoulder at the empty doorway. "You were outside just as long as me, and I had a blanket. You can't be feeling great, either."

"I'm more accustomed to this kind of thing. I'll be all right."

Shaun found a few pillows in the cupboard where he'd found the candles, and tucked one behind her head so she could remain upright and comfortable. Several others he tucked around her back and sides.

"I'll go as quickly as I can," he said, planting a kiss on her cheek. "Keep quiet and I'll be back in a jiff. If you hear anything out there, whatever it is, *don't come out*. Stay here. I will come back for you."

Lexie nodded, exhaustion plain on her face. What had he been thinking, dragging her into this? She'd had enough to deal with from that initial attack on the parking deck, and yet he'd gone and pulled her the rest of the way into this fight— a fight that wasn't hers and shouldn't be hers. Yet, if he hadn't, they might not have spent all these hours together, and he never would have learned what a resilient and tender heart she possessed.

With a prayer that God would see him through this one way or the other, Shaun drew his gun, peeked around the corner and looked back at Lexie, sitting peacefully on the floor.

"I'll be just a few minutes," he said, mustering a weak smile.

"You'd better," she said, a teasing sparkle in her tired voice. "If you think I'm going to let you disappear on me after *that*, you're sorely mistaken."

Shaun exited the room with a burst of speed, heading directly for where he assumed the stairs would be. With the main elevator out of the equation, he didn't want to risk the maintenance elevator in case they were tied together on the same electrical system.

Despite the surrounding darkness, Shaun's eyes had become conditioned enough to the near-absence of light that he maintained sure footing until he found the stairs. He threw open the door and took the steps three at a time, pushing his lungs to the point of exhaustion. He'd given Lexie the impression of being more certain of her safety than he actually felt, though she had to know that. The woman had a remarkable head on her shoulders. *And soft lips, too.*

Lips that, Lord willing, he'd be kissing again and again once this whole thing ended. He had at least a month's worth of vacation time coming to him, and while he'd been planning to use it on a beach somewhere in the South Pacific, maybe he could hang around the rocky shores of Newfoundland for a few coffee dates with Lexie. If she was willing to spend time with him, of course.

Shaun blinked against the bright lights of the main deck, eyes aching at the shift after so many hours in darkness and silence. The air around him was anything but silent—noise and laughter filtered down the hall to where he stood. The sound came from the direction of the lounge, loud enough for Shaun to suspect that the room had filled with passengers evacuated from the affected areas on the lower decks…if there had even been passengers down there at all. The place had seemed deserted.

When he thought it through, it made sense, particularly if their pursuer wanted to be certain that the only casualties were himself and Lexie.

No passengers…because passengers would ask questions. Cause the ship to be shut down, maybe delay service while an investigation was underway to solve the crime. Customers would have to choose Atlantic Voyages' competitor in the meantime. But an isolated incident with no witnesses? Much easier to shove under the rug or explain away.

That meant the Wolf's identity matched that of someone invested in the ongoing success of this particular ferry service. Atlantic Voyages' competitor must not be a viable option for criminal activities, which spun the compass directly toward the few people who could arrange things like GPS trackers in walkie-talkies or an extremely isolated bomb blast. Who had the authority to arrange for no passengers to be on the lower deck before the bomb went off? And why bother with such an elaborate scheme? Josh's walkie-talkie had been missing, but pegging him as the Wolf? Josh didn't fit the profile, but then, what did Shaun really know about the notorious criminal beyond the bare bones of how he conducted his operation?

The Wolf hadn't escaped detection for a decade

by allowing evidence to clearly point to his identity. He wasn't a sloppy man by any means, and the missing walkie-talkie from Josh's belt was an amateur mistake. Sure, they had the Wolf running scared, but that had been *far* too overt. Almost like a last-ditch effort at deflection.

Shaun rounded the corner to the security office, mind racing and hoping that Lexie wouldn't have to sit alone in the dark much longer. He picked up speed and sprinted the rest of the way to Parsons's office. Shaun gripped the corner of the door frame and came to an abrupt stop, startling the head of ferry security as he sat at his desk, typing on a computer.

"Parsons! My radio is toast. I need yours. We have to radio in medical and send them to deck three. Lexie's hurt and she needs attention immediately."

Parsons jumped up from his desk, quickly shifting papers around with a look of utter shock on his face. "Lane! We thought—I mean—the bomb! And then we didn't hear from you. The woman, is she…"

"Lexie's okay, she just needs help." Now that he'd stopped moving, Shaun's lungs had caught up to him. He doubled over, resting his hands on his knees. "And she needs it fast. Might be frostbite. The sooner we get medical to her, the less likely she'll be to lose a finger or toe."

Parsons frowned and grabbed a handful of papers off his desk, shoving them into a drawer that he locked with a key on his belt. "You all right, son? You look like you've been through the ringer."

"Lexie." Shaun wheezed, drawing deep breaths. "Go ahead. I'll find the other guys and let them know what's going on. I assume they're dealing with fallout from the blast?"

"Yes, of course. I'll deal with Lexie. Don't worry. Third floor, you said?"

"In the prayer chapel." Shaun released a deep breath, his lungs finally starting to calm. "Have medical bring a stretcher. She's feisty, but she's weaker than she'll let on. Probably try to run a marathon tomorrow if we let her."

"Roger." Parsons pulled a walkie-talkie from a wall mount and handed it to Shaun as he headed out the door. "You need a sec?"

"Yeah. I'll shut the door behind me, don't worry." With a grunt, Parsons sauntered off, a little less speed in his step than Shaun would have liked. He stood a little straighter to call after the man and reiterate the need for expediency. "Say, Parsons—" Shaun's words froze in his throat as his gaze swept across Parsons's office. In the far corner of the room, on the top shelf next to a tackle box and a rusty-looking dive helmet, sat a display box of antique hunting knives.

That's not so strange, Shaun thought, shaking off the immediate alarm. *Plenty of people keep antiques.* Having it placed on a shelf next to old gear only told him Parsons was sentimental, not a criminal. If it was a crime to own old wilderness equipment, someone should have arrested Shaun's father a long time ago.

Shaun chastised himself for wasting time with absurd speculation. He needed to be on the move, find the other guys and figure out how to confront Josh regarding his suspicions. Shaun reached in to grab the door handle, pulled the door halfway shut and froze again. Directly across from him, peeking out of the top of the drawer Parsons had just shoved papers into and locked, was a slip of red.

With his visual acuity honed through years of training, the flash of color stood out to Shaun in an otherwise understated but messy room. It looked as if something inside the drawer had been displaced when Parsons shoved his handful of papers inside. Shaun released his hold on the door handle and stepped into the office, light-headedness creeping up his spine and into his skull.

Using two fingers, Shaun grasped the red paper. It was firm and stiff. *Like a folder.* He tugged on it, hearing the sound of tearing from inside the drawer. The drawer had locked, but the lock was now jammed on the folder. No problem. What kind of CIA agent would he be if he didn't know how to pick a simple lock?

It took all of thirty seconds for Shaun to open the drawer and pull out the folder. He realized with surprise that his hands were trembling. Inside his gut, he knew exactly what would be inside this folder once he opened it—but he desperately hoped he was wrong, because if this folder was what he thought it might be, he'd been very, *very* wrong this whole time.

It took a fraction of a second to confirm his suspicions. Instantly, all the pieces fell into place. With a burst of adrenaline, Shaun raced through the door to follow Parsons—only to find himself nearly face-to-face with Reed.

"We need to find Lexie," Shaun shouted as he ran full tilt toward Reed. "She's in—"

Reed's arm shot out, clotheslining Shaun as he tried to run past. Shaun tumbled to the floor, clutching his throat. He rolled and came up in a crouch, but the combination of shock and surprise had thrown him off his game, putting Reed in an advantageous position. Shaun reached behind him to grab his gun, only to see it lying on the floor three feet away. It had fallen out of his belt when he went down—and Reed saw it, too.

A million scenarios swept through Shaun's brain, but only one of them left him alive at the end. Rather than take Reed on in a diving match for the gun, Shaun rushed his opponent, fist ready to swing, but being clotheslined had lowered his reaction time.

Reed landed the first punch, and Shaun's vision faded to darkness.

SEVENTEEN

Lexie shivered in the candlelit prayer room. She wasn't blind—she'd seen the fear on Shaun's face. He worried that she'd lose a finger or toe after being outside for too long, and Lexie couldn't blame him. But after the way he'd kissed her and told her it would be okay, she believed him. Despite everything that had happened so far, he still trusted in God's ultimate control. She didn't know if she'd take it quite that far just yet...but she was working on it. Actively. Like, right now.

A soft rustle in the hallway sent alarm bells ringing. Could that be Shaun? When the rustle stopped and no further sound came, her heart skipped a beat. No, not Shaun. Suddenly, the light from the candles seemed overwhelmingly bright. Surely someone would be able to see that from the doorway. She should snuff them out.

With aching fingers, Lexie picked up the candles one by one and blew them out with a quick huff, her lips as close to the flames as she could get them without burning. The smell of extinguished flame wafted through her corner of the room.

Seconds later, the rustle returned. The footsteps were more distinct this time. Lexie held her breath as they came closer and closer.

A bright light shone from the doorway into Lexie's face, and she squinted up into it. Not Shaun, but at least whoever had the light hadn't shot her on sight.

"Miss Reilly," said a familiar voice. "There you are. I hear you're injured?"

Who was it? She couldn't see past the light. "Yes…did Shaun send you?"

"Not exactly." The beam of light moved off her face, allowing her to see clearly around the gleam. Josh stood in the doorway, flashlight in one hand and stun gun in the other, the latter pointed directly at her. "But I suggest you come with me. I'm afraid I won't take no for an answer."

Lexie hauled herself to her feet, wincing at the ache in her leg. She'd been so cold, she'd forgotten all about the bullet that had grazed her leg while she and Shaun were on the run. "I'm not going anywhere without Shaun. He'll be back at any second, and he's bringing the rest of security with him."

To her surprise, instead of capitulating, Josh only laughed. "He thinks so, does he? Then that should make the next few minutes very interesting. Come on, out of the room. No funny stuff."

His casual dismissal of the rest of the security team stunned Lexie worse than she thought any stun gun could. Josh waved the gun at the doorway, and despite the typical nonlethal nature of stun guns, Lexie knew very well that the tool could be deadly in the wrong hands. She had no illusions about how much it would hurt to be shot, or that she'd walk away from a high-voltage dose of pure electricity unscathed.

In the hallway, Josh gripped her forearm and pointed her in the direction that she and Shaun had come from. Josh used the flashlight to guide their way, but Lexie paid very little attention to where he led them. Her mind raced, trying to make sense of his words. Did he have an accomplice on the security team? Perhaps he and Reed had been operating right under Parsons's nose. It made sense, except that neither man seemed as if he had the strength or skill to pull off such a complex operation under their boss's nose. Then again, what did she and Shaun really know about them? All she'd seen from these men was a willingness to follow orders.

"How'd you know where to find me?" Lexie blinked against the rising wave of panic. She needed to stall whatever inevitable fate Josh had planned for her.

"I smelled the smoke from the candles you put out. Thanks for that, by the way."

"Where are you taking me?"

"You'll see," he mumbled. "Quiet, please."

"You'll never get away with this. You already know the ship is stuck in the ice and the Coast Guard is on the way. Passengers will need to return to their rooms to get their belongings, and someone's going to see something."

"This will be long over by then, Reilly. I'm pleased to say that this little operation is in its final throes. It'll be over soon and you won't have to worry about a thing."

Everything he said made less and less sense. "Why? Are you going to kill me and finish off the job?"

"Kill you? Whatever gave you that idea?" They'd come to a stop in front of a familiar-looking metal door with a crash bar in the center. "Outside, please."

Lexie's semi-warmed bones grew chilled again. "I just came in from outside. Please, I might have frostbite already."

"I think frostbite is going to be the least of your worries." He chuckled. It was a chilling sound, and for the first time since Shaun had left her alone to find help, Lexie wondered whether she'd actually make it out of this alive. Where was Shaun? Had Josh already "taken care" of him upstairs? Was he lying somewhere in the dark, in need of medical assistance?

"I said, outside." Josh shoved her from behind, forcing Lexie to push on the crash bar and open the door. To Lexie's surprise, she wasn't blasted by cold night air but might as well have been stepping into a bowl of pea soup. Thick, early morning fog enveloped them from every side. Lexie could barely see her hands in front of her face, let alone Josh behind her. If only she could get him to release her arm somehow.

"My leg hurts," she said. "I can't stand for long. You shot me in the leg earlier, and I think I've lost some blood."

"I didn't shoot you," Josh grunted. "Keep quiet if you know what's good for you."

"Of course you did. What I don't understand is how—"

"I said, *quiet.* I won't ask again." The stun gun pressed painfully into her spine. A radio's alarm broke the silence of the morning air, and Lexie heard Josh slide a walkie-talkie from his belt. "I've got her. We're outside on deck three. South end."

A garbled response that sounded like "be right there" came over the line. Moments later, the door reopened. Lexie held her breath, praying for Shaun to burst through the fog, gun drawn—

Parsons slipped into view instead. Seeing Josh, he raised his hands in surrender.

"Watch out!" Lexie shrieked at Parsons, hoping the man would turn around and run back inside. "He's armed and dangerous! And he's a—"

Behind her, Josh groaned in exasperation. Not the reaction she'd expected. Nor had she expected Parsons to ignore her, cross the short distance to them with a bemused expression on his face and point a lazy finger at Josh. "Him? He's a what?"

"An internationally wanted criminal mastermind…" Lexie's voice trailed off as she saw the cruel smirk on Parsons's face. Also gone was the friendly Newfy accent. "No. Oh, no, no, *no*."

Parsons nodded. "I'm afraid so, little lady. Thank you, Bosworth, I'll take it from here."

"The CIA agent?" Josh growled.

"He's been dealt with, but the icebreaker is nearly here. We need to wrap this up if we're going to move these women when we dock. We've had—" he glanced pointedly at Lexie "—a number of unexpected complications on this journey."

Lexie gasped, drawing Parsons's attention back to herself. "You're working for Josh? Don't you understand? He's trafficking young women and forcing them into domestic slavery and grueling overseas factory work. Doesn't that make you sick?"

Parsons shrugged, glanced at Josh and laughed. "No, not really. In fact, it makes me a very, very rich man."

Deeper understanding dawned on Lexie. Parsons didn't work for Josh. *Josh worked for him.* "But…"

"I believe you know me as the Wolf, Alexandra. Now, that's quite enough exposition for one day. Hand her over, Bosworth." Parsons gestured at Josh, wiggling his fingers. "I need to pack this one away with the others and dispose of a body. Chop, chop. Work to be done."

Lexie's heart sank into her shoes. This truly was the end after all. They'd dispose of her and Shaun, and neither one of them would be seen again. The missing-persons investigator would become a missing person. Then Parsons's words dawned on her. "Wait, pack me away? What do you mean? Are you going to kill me?"

Parsons raised an eyebrow and clapped his hands. "Kill you? Of course not. I haven't killed you despite all your nosing around, so why should I do it now?"

Lexie sputtered in disbelief. "The bomb? The shots? You gassed us and one of your men attacked us in the engine room! Of course you've been trying to kill us."

"Uh-uh." Parsons wagged a finger in her face. "Not true. The man who attacked you paid for his mistake, and the others? Carefully timed and controlled to ensure that you'd be returned to me in one piece. *You*, that is. Lane, I couldn't care less about. Collateral damage, really. I'm not a stupid man, Alexandra."

Lexie's heart thudded against her ribs. Why was this happening? "But Shaun said you rescued us from the gas in the library. Why do that if you set it up in the first place? Why bother?"

"Why? Use your noggin, girl. I needed to gain your trust to find out what you knew. And to stay in the loop to keep you from getting too close." He winked, and Lexie felt nauseated. "Besides, it took me off your suspect list from the very beginning. Simple as that."

A wave of heat washed over Lexie as a ringing in her ears signaled the beginning of a panic attack. She had no one to help calm her down this time, no one to make sure she was safe. If the panic attack took full hold, she'd be vulnerable for at least ten minutes until it passed.

God, help me, please. It was the second sincere prayer she'd offered up since Shaun's departure for help. And although she still wasn't sure if God truly cared, Shaun believed that God was in control, that He had a purpose and a plan for all things, even in the darkest hours and the remotest corners of the earth. Isn't that what she'd been meant to learn in Botswana all those years ago? Isn't that what God was still trying to teach her, even now?

She closed her eyes and took a deep breath as Parsons continued his diatribe.

"You should have left well enough alone, and I would have allowed you to return home without incident. Your problem is, you're too nosy for your own good."

Lexie struggled against Josh's grip, but the stun gun jabbed into her spine. "You're a monster. How can you do this to innocent people? You're destroying families. Ruining lives. Those girls have a bright future ahead of them."

"Big corporations destroy thousands of lives—millions, you might argue—every day in subtler ways, and no one complains about that, do they? And besides, these women still have a bright future. They'll be helping local economies on a daily basis, increasing economic output in the factories they work for. It's still a bright future, just not the one you so mistakenly think they'll give themselves if they have the free will to do so. Most people lack ambition, Alexandra. You're one of the rare few who still have it—but we'll break it out of you soon enough."

Lexie's blood ran cold. "Break it out of me? Never. Might as well kill me now." She hoped her effort at false confidence hid the tremor in her voice.

Parsons laughed again, and Lexie's stomach roiled. "And lose out on a potential sale? Of course not. You may be feisty, but we have methods for dealing with that. You're young, strong, in good health. You'll fetch a pretty penny at one of the brick building camps."

Acid built up in Lexie's throat and she swallowed it down. The man was insane. Selling women to work in factories? Shaun had been right—cutting off Maria's braid meant keeping the person intact, so she could be worked harder at a greater profit. It was beyond sickening. "You'll never get away with this," she hissed.

"I will, and I do. Have been for many, many years." Parsons motioned at Josh to hand her over. "I'll take it from here, Bosworth. Good work, as usual."

But to Lexie's utter shock, the stun gun's pressure against her back eased as Josh turned the gun on Parsons. "I don't think so. This has gone far enough."

It was Parsons's turn to be surprised. "What's this? You want a bigger cut? We can negotiate that. You haven't been around as long as Reed and Walter—oh, right, Walter is no longer with us—but normally we do this behind closed doors, much more civilly."

"Not a raise. Timothy Parsons, turn around and put your hands in the air."

Lexie stifled a gasp. Who *was* this guy?

Parsons voiced the exact same sentiment, raising his hands up, palms toward Josh. "You may be overstepping your bounds here a bit, son."

"Miss Reilly, please step behind me." Josh didn't turn to look at Lexie, but she did what he asked, because…why not? Getting out of the line of fire sounded good, unless this was just another ruse to try and goad her into information or stop her from running.

Josh lowered his voice to speak to her. "You need to trust me. I'm a deep cover agent from the RCMP. I've been working the same ring as Lane, from the inside. I've been feeding information to the CIA for several years now, but when you began your search for Maria, I realized we had the girl en route and there was a possibility you might be able to free her before she got moved overseas. I'd hoped you and Lane would cross paths."

Lexie could hardly believe her ears—and neither could Parsons, by the looks of it. The man's cheeks had grown red, his brow dark and furrowed.

"I don't believe you," growled Parsons. "You've worked for me for almost a year and haven't done a thing."

"Wasn't the right time. I needed solid evidence and the right people to take you down."

"You're not that good."

"I only had to be better than you. And thankfully, Miss Reilly and Agent Lane were the right people."

Parsons's scowl deepened. "You got a badge you can show me? I'll go peacefully, but I need to know you're not lying. That you're not part of some rival group looking to scam in on my good thing here."

Josh chuckled. "Good news, Mr. Parsons. I packed my badge this morning, for a moment just like this." Josh reached inside his shirt pocket, but that was all the distraction Parsons needed. With Josh's split focus, Parsons reached behind his back and drew a pistol, firing off a shot before Josh knew what had hit him.

Lexie watched, stunned, as the RCMP officer crumpled face-first to the ground. Almost immediately, a rivulet of blood seeped out from underneath the body, traversing the icy surface of the deck.

"That takes care of that," said Parsons, turning his gun on Lexie. "Never liked that guy anyway. Didn't respect the ocean the way I do, you understand? I may have ulterior motives, but I love this boat. It's like a second home—well, first home, really."

The man was delusional. Completely deranged. There could be no other explanation. Lexie could barely believe this was the same man they'd worked side-by-side with for the past two days, but then again, hadn't they had clues? Always knowing where she and Shaun would be and when, and then the tracker inside the walkie-talkie…of *course* it had been him. He'd probably tracked them on his computer—a computer in the security office that he had access to at all times. How had they not seen this coming? He'd been clever, rescuing them from the gas incident.

She glanced down at Josh. He hadn't moved. "He needs a doctor," Lexie cried, the buzzing in her ears growing louder. "He'll die."

Parsons shrugged. "That's the idea. But that's what I have Reed for. Cleanup duty. He should be here any minute now. I imagine Lane got the surprise of his life, eh? Or should I say, the *last* surprise of his life."

Lexie squeezed her eyes shut and willed the tears and panic away. Now was not the time. The man in front of her so clearly viewed people as objects that he'd shot Josh in cold blood. Doubtless he'd do the same to her if she caused too much trouble. Still, he'd intentionally kept her alive this far, so she might have a fighting chance.

But this time, she'd have to face the fight alone.

She found herself longing to see Shaun, just one more time. Had she and Shaun met again after eight years, only to lose each other? Even during their kiss, she hadn't been fully sure of herself, but now she knew. If she had even one more moment with Shaun, she'd tell him exactly how she felt. Her head, though resistant to the truth he'd shared with her, could be overcome—because her heart, despite it all, had fallen hard for him.

Please, Lord. I don't know what to do, but I trust You've brought me here for a purpose. I do believe that. I trust You.

Parsons crossed the remaining stretch of deck toward her, stepping carefully across the still-icy surface. He pulled Josh's radio off the immobile man's belt and opened a channel. "Hey, Reed? You on your way?"

And then she heard it. A soft click of a latch nearby, too quiet to be Parsons's accomplice heading out onto the deck. Hastily, Lexie cleared her throat, hoping it would cover the sound. "Can't see much of anything out there today, can we?" She focused her attention out toward the foggy sea, shuffling the short distance to the railing. "How will you know when the icebreaker gets here? What if you run out of time to clean up?"

Parsons kept his gun out, but lazily waved it in the direction of the ocean. "We'll hear it. I'll get word from the captain as soon as they're in striking distance—the captain trusts me, of course." He winked at Lexie. "I'll have plenty of time to get this place cleaned—"

Suddenly, out of the mist, Shaun swooped in like a falcon. He targeted Parsons's gun and struck the man's arm with an expertly aimed blow, knocking the weapon out of Parsons's hand. Parsons jumped for it as it flew out of his hand and over the railing, but the deck was far too icy for that kind of sudden movement. Instead of jumping upward as intended, his feet slipped on the ice, pitching him forward across the railing.

The railing's slick coating of ice proved problematic to hold on to, and though Parsons gripped the bar, his bulky frame tipped over the edge of the rail as Shaun lunged to grab any part of the man. Anything to stop him from falling over the side of the ship. Shaun caught Parsons's wrist as the man struggled to hold on to the slippery, frozen surface.

"You're not going down that easily," Shaun bellowed, face flushed with the effort of trying to keep the big man's grasp from failing. One of Shaun's feet slipped, and he stumbled to regain his balance. Another slip like that, and he'd disappear over the side with the man he struggled to save.

Panic threatened to overwhelm Lexie, and she sank to her knees as Shaun fought to keep hold of the larger man. The ache in her calf pulsed with the sting of a fresh wound, and the buzzing in her ears nearly drowned out the sound of everything around her.

"You've ruined everything," Parsons huffed,

breaths coming short as his left hand slid, finger by finger, from the railing. "I'll kill you for this."

"You were going to kill me anyway," Shaun said.

They were both going to fail. Lexie's throat constricted with fear, but if she didn't act, they'd lose everything. With one final prayer for strength, she reached up to grip Shaun around his legs, giving him leverage on the slippery deck. If she could ground him with even more weight somehow, he might be able to pull Parsons back aboard—

"I'm losing him," Shaun called. "Lexie, I can't hold on!"

Lexie released Shaun and leaped to her feet. She reached over the railing, trying to grab Parsons's left hand, but the man's loose arm flailed too much, his weight too heavy to reach back up and take the lifeline Lexie offered.

"Come on," Shaun grunted through gritted teeth. "Reach! You can do it!"

Parsons, to Lexie's confusion, began to laugh. Shaun's sudden intake of breath brought her attention to where Shaun still gripped Parsons, and noticed the slide of skin against skin. Shaun was losing his grip, and there was nothing either of them could do about it.

"Just let go." Parsons sneered. "You know you want to. You're no hero, Lane. It's over for me."

"No!" Shaun leaned farther over the railing to

adjust his grip, but like a scene played in slow motion, Shaun's feet slipped again on the deck surface. Lexie launched herself at him, wrapping her arms around his torso to keep him solidly on the deck, even as Parsons's hand slid the final inch from Shaun's grasp.

With a shout, Parsons plummeted through the air, four stories down the side of the ferry toward the thick ice below.

Lexie stared, watching Parsons fall, until Shaun pulled her into his chest and covered her face. A thud and a crack signified the end.

And as much as Lexie wanted to breathe a sigh of relief, to scream in frustration and to cry in sadness all at once, she couldn't. They had three girls to find.

EIGHTEEN

Shaun loosened his grip on Lexie and held her at arm's length, her beautiful face in his hands. "I thought I'd lost you," he said, pulling her back into his arms before she could protest.

"We need to find them," she whispered. "We promised."

His relief at seeing Lexie had been palpable, and as much as he wanted to stand there and hold her forever now that the threat of danger had passed, she was right. There were still three young women aboard who needed their help, one of whom might require medical attention.

"You can tell me how you found me later," Lexie said, pulling away. She ran over to Josh's side and crouched, pressing two fingers against his neck. "He's alive, but his pulse is weak. Call medical."

"Already on it." Shaun stepped carefully and quickly across the deck to use one of the emergency phones, grateful they were still working. The medical team arrived in a matter of minutes and tended to the wounded RCMP officer with practiced speed.

"We should go," Lexie said. "One of the nurses is going to come with us, but we still don't know where the girls are."

Shaun tapped the side of his nose. "If I were relocating abductees on a ship, I'd keep them far, far away from other people as much as possible. What better way to do that than hiding them in a room that the people searching for them have already checked?"

"You think they're back in the engine room?" Lexie eyed him with skepticism.

"I think that's the best place to start."

With one of the nurses in tow, Lexie led the way from the outside deck back through the darkened halls, finding the stairs with only a little guidance from the nurse. Lexie and Shaun flew down the steps to the engine room. The door had been locked.

"That's a good sign," Shaun said as he stepped back and slammed a donkey kick into the spot above the door handle. The door swung open with a bang. "Good thing they don't pay much attention to maintenance on anything down here aside from the engines."

Lexie rushed past him into the dimly lit room. The rumble of the engines didn't stop Lexie from calling out to the girls by name.

At first, all they heard was the continuous thrum of rumbling engine power, but then a faint, rhythmic banging joined the wall of sound.

"At the back," Shaun said. "It's coming from the back."

They sprinted to the back of the engine room as the bangs grew louder. Through a gray door, almost invisible against the wall's matching gray paint, came muffled shouts.

Lexie ran to the door, Shaun hot on her heels.

"It's locked," Lexie moaned, banging her fist on a hefty lock across the handle. "Now what? Where do we get a master key?"

Shaun leaned in and kissed the top of her head. "I've got this. I'm a superspy, after all," he whispered. The smile she gave him in return warmed him to the tips of his toes. He'd done it. *They'd* done it. And now they were going to finish it.

After an agonizing two minutes, he felt and heard the soft click of the lock's release. He stepped back as Lexie pulled open the door, revealing three young women huddled together.

The nurse dashed in to assist Jamie, who wore a makeshift bandage around her upper leg.

"Are we safe?" asked Maria, blinking away the darkness of the cramped closet. Shaun recognized her from the photograph.

"Everything's going to be all right now," Lexie said, rushing forward to wrap the girl up in her arms. "Everything is going to be all right from now on." She looked over the top of Maria's head at Shaun, relief and gratitude in her eyes.

It was finally over.

Back in the captain's quarters, Shaun observed Lexie from afar as she chatted with the three rescued young women. Despite Reed's initial advantage when Shaun had encountered him outside of Parsons's office, the security officer's on-the-job combat training had been no match for Shaun's Agency-trained skills. Reed's first blow had knocked the wind out of him, but within a matter of minutes, Shaun had incapacitated Reed and convinced him to admit his part in the scheme. Parsons's call through the walkie-talkie had only confirmed Shaun's findings, and the GPS tracker inside the radio—which Parsons's computer held the tracking program for—had told him exactly where to find Lexie.

Shaun returned his attention to the phone, where Jack yammered away about what protocol to follow once the Coast Guard arrived on the ice-breaker.

"You said the RCMP informant is stabilized?" Jack asked, Jolly Rancher candy clacking against his teeth.

"That's right. He's not entirely out of the brambles, but there's an RCMP evacuation helicopter standing by to swoop in as soon as the fog lifts."

"Good. Can't believe the way this played out, Agent. Incredible."

Shaun chuckled, shaking his head. "I can barely believe it myself, Jack. God had His hand in it the whole time. Look, I should get back to Lexie and the girls. Check in with you later? The ice-breaker is almost here, so we'll be back en route in a few hours."

Shaun's finger hovered over the button to end the call, when he heard a shout from the other end of the line. He pulled the receiver back up to his ear. "What now?"

"*Hrrmph.* Think you'd be a little more grateful to the guy giving you big news."

"Come on, spit it out." Shaun knew that tone of voice. The case officer had information he couldn't wait to tell him.

"Looked into those names you mentioned. A file came up for one of the Reilly women."

Shaun's stomach twinged. Was this something he wanted to know? Had he done the right thing by asking Jack to dig for information?

"The older sibling, Nikki, right?"

"Yes, that's right." Shaun's blood ran cold.

"Full name Nicola Grace Reilly, yeah? Turns out one of our teams picked her up as part of a bust for a similar op six years ago. We had her under agency protection to testify against her captor, and kept her around as a possible asset for future trafficking cases afterward. In theory, that part was voluntary, but you know what *that* means with the Agency sometimes. Anyway, for some reason the files for her and several other witnesses were reopened not twenty minutes ago when you called in. There'll be a lot of paperwork before she and the other protected witnesses can get back to their normal lives and families, but she's alive and—according to the record in front of me—in good health."

Shaun thanked Jack and hung up, shock ricocheting through his system. Lexie's sister was *alive*.

Fighting to suppress a nervous grin, he crossed the room and tapped Lexie on the shoulder. "Can I interrupt for a moment?" Maria and the girls excused themselves, so he took a seat across from Lexie and clasped her hands between his. "I have some news, but first, how are you doing?"

Lexie shivered despite the warmth of the room, pulling her hands from his to wrap them around her middle. "I got an all clear from the nurse for now, but they'll give me a full checkup once we reach the island. Just in case."

Shaun shook his head and ran his fingers through his hair. "I didn't mean your health, Lexie."

She shrugged and smiled at him under her eyelashes. "I know. I guess I'm all right, but there are still a few things I don't understand. Like, how did you find me?"

"Parsons's GPS tracking program helped, but so did this." He reached into his pocket and pulled out a delicate, silver object. He took Lexie's hand back and dropped her silver Nikki bracelet into the center. "Took a cue from the missing girls and the earring, did you?"

Lexie grinned and clasped her fingers around the bracelet. "I thought it might help you to know I didn't leave on my own."

"You thought right."

"But what about Reed? Parsons said he'd come after you to take care of things."

"In case you haven't noticed, I'm kind of durable. Takes a lot to keep this lumberjack down." He winked and tugged at the corner of his plaid shirt. "Yeah, I know that's what you've been thinking."

Lexie laughed and shifted her position to lay her head on Shaun's shoulder. "Just because you have terrible fashion sense—or just a bad ability to disguise yourself, I haven't quite figured that out—doesn't mean I like you any less."

"Oh?" Shaun pulled away, forcing Lexie to lift her head. "Is that an admission I hear? You actually like me? To what do I owe this revelation?"

Lexie rolled her eyes, though her smile remained. "Don't count your chickens, Lane. I just can't believe this is over."

His grin returned, and he wrapped his arm around her shoulders. "Everything except for a few loose ends, it seems."

"Loose ends?" It was Lexie's turn to pull away from him. "Whatever on earth do you mean by that?"

He cleared his throat, trusting God for the right words to say. "Your sister. She's alive and has been under—all right, I'll just say it—CIA protection for a number of years. It would've been too risky to allow her to contact her family, but I imagine you'll hear from her soon."

Lexie's jaw dropped and she gasped, her eyes immediately filling with tears. "You can't be serious."

He nodded, and that was all the confirmation she needed. He drew her close again and let the waves of emotion carry her away. After a time, she lifted her head, a shy smile curving the corners of her rosy lips. "So, now what? Where does this leave us?"

Shaun frowned in confusion before recognizing the true, unspoken question behind her words. "That's the other loose end. You and me. But I'm ready to figure it out. With you, Lexie. Only you."

Lexie's cheeks turned pink as Shaun planted a kiss on the crown of her head. She laid her head back on Shaun's shoulder, releasing a sigh of contentment that brought a wave of pure joy to Shaun's heart. "If that's the only loose end left to make sense of? I'm okay with that. I trust you."

EPILOGUE

"You've got some nerve bringing me here." Lexie laughed, stepping one foot at a time into the rocky canoe. "I thought we promised no more boats."

"We did, but I'd hoped you'd make an exception for it this time." Shaun held her hand as she got seated before passing her a gray wool blanket. "For your lap, in case you get cold."

"Did you steal this from the ferry?" Shaun only winked in response. Gazing around, Lexie took in the beauty of Lake Ontario at sunset. Reds, yellows and oranges sparkled over the surface of the water, the air cool and pleasantly crisp with the onset of autumn. The trees and landscape along the water's edge were turning early shades of the sunset's brilliant palette.

Lexie took a deep breath and released it slowly, savoring the peace that came with healed bruises—both hers and those of the people she cared about. While there would always be more people to find, it had been so beautiful to see Maria and the other missing young women reunited with their families. Even more incredible, Nikki was flying in to visit next week. Lexie had learned that Nikki had spent her time under CIA protection attending a community college and obtaining her teacher's license. Nikki now spent her days in a position of responsibility as a teacher's aide in a Fairfax County, Virginia, elementary school. Lexie had so many questions for Nikki, but before any of that, she planned to give her sister the biggest hug of her life and not let go for a long, long time. She'd even organized a big family celebration for Nikki's arrival and, to Lexie's surprise and delight, when they'd spoken on the phone her sister had hinted that she might be interested in doing a little house-hunting during her visit.

Although the end of the case had meant Shaun needed to return to Langley, Virginia, to wrap up details of his years-long operation, Lexie had been fortunate enough to meet up with him several times for dinner on Newfoundland when the ship finally harbored. Those long conversations and heartfelt talks had been a whirlwind of a different kind, sending them both down a path they'd wanted to tread, though still rife with uncertainty. He'd managed to fly up to spend a Saturday afternoon with her at least once a month since then, but even with video chats added to the mix, it wasn't enough.

Lexie simply wasn't sure how to proceed. She couldn't ask Shaun to leave his job, his work was far too important to far too many people. As much as they loved each other, lately she'd been worried that perhaps weekend visits were as far as their futures would take them.

"Are you comfortable?" Shaun asked, concern in his eyes. "Something's bothering you."

She shrugged. "This is wonderful, Shaun. Perfect, even—despite the boat."

"But you're worried about something." He reached across and took her hands in his.

Lexie sighed. "We've been through so much together, Shaun, and these past few months have been great, but…"

"You know I love you, right?" Shaun gingerly leaned forward to kiss her forehead, taking care not to rock their little boat. "You're the most incredible woman I've ever met, strong in ways I couldn't even imagine a person could be until I met you."

"I love you, too," she said, savoring the words, even though they'd been said before. They felt different tonight, though—more potent. She wasn't the only one worried about something. Shaun kept looking around as though he expected a horde of bad guys to pop out of the water or drop on them from an airplane. "It's just that, well…"

"It's hard being apart most of the time and you

want more?" Lexie gaped at his mind-reading prowess, but Shaun just shrugged and ran his fingers through his floppier-than-ever hair. "Wasn't hard to figure out. It's because I feel the same way. Six months is long enough to get to know each other at our stage in life. It's time to make things more permanent."

Lexie rolled her eyes. "You're so romantic, Shaun. But I don't see how this is going to work."

He raised one eyebrow and knelt on the floor of the boat. Lexie's heart caught in her throat. Was he actually… He wasn't. Was he?

"I know exactly how it's going to work, Alexandra Reilly." He reached into his pocket, took her wrist and turned it palm-up—just as he'd done after saving her life on the ferry's parking deck. His fingers shook as he placed a shimmering diamond ring into her hand. "If you'll agree to marry me, that is."

Lexie's breath came in short bursts. "Of course I will, Shaun, but—"

"Do you trust me?"

She pouted at the implication. "Of course I do."

"Then say yes."

It was true—she did trust him. Who would have thought that after twelve years, she and Shaun Carver would reunite, both of them so incredibly different people after all this time. He had a dedication and faith that she aspired to, and there was no doubt in her mind that he could find a way to make this work for the both of them. If there was anyone in the world who understood her work, it was he—and vice versa.

"Yes, then. I will marry you."

With a shout of joy, Shaun drew her face down to his and kissed her with a fire he knew would only grow with time. "Then how about this—you working as a missing-persons consultant for the CIA. Start an American branch of your company. We'll make a difference together."

The joy that welled up inside of her was uncontainable, and she kissed him back. They laughed as the boat rocked back and forth, which they quickly stabilized with a bit of patience and teamwork…the same way they'd solved their problems in the past, and the same way they would tackle them together in the future.

* * * * *

Dear Reader,

Thanks so much for keeping company with Lexie and Shaun while they were stuck in the ice. The journey from North Sydney, Nova Scotia, to Argentia, Newfoundland, is actually quite a beautiful trip when the weather is right! I grew up in Nova Scotia, so the maritime setting is quite close to my heart. Cold weather, though? Not so much.

Like Lexie, I've had moments in my life when I learned that people close to me were not who they portrayed themselves to be. It hurts when people don't live up to our expectations, but ultimately we are only responsible for our own choices. The good news is God can use any situation for His glory.

I believe that God brings the right people into our lives when we need them the most. Shaun and Lexie never expected to cross each other's paths again, but when they did, the timing was right. It allowed them to be a stronger force for good than they could have ever been apart, despite the difficulties they had to work through to get there. Sometimes it's those rock-bottom moments in life that shape us and mold us the most, and they usually happen when we least expect it. I hope that when those moments come for you, you're able to take a deep breath and remember that God is always in control.

I love to hear from readers, so please come visit me at michellekarl.com, or drop me an email at michellekarl@gmail.com.

Blessings,
Michelle

LARGER-PRINT BOOKS!

GET 2 FREE LARGER-PRINT NOVELS PLUS 2 FREE MYSTERY GIFTS

Love Inspired

Larger-print novels are now available...

LILPDIR13R

REQUEST YOUR FREE BOOKS!
2 FREE WHOLESOME ROMANCE NOVELS IN LARGER PRINT
PLUS 2
FREE
MYSTERY GIFTS

🌾🌾🌾🌾🌾🌾🌾🌾🌾🌾🌾🌾🌾🌾🌾🌾🌾🌾🌾🌾

HEARTWARMING™

Wholesome, tender romances

YES! Please send me 2 FREE Harlequin® Heartwarming Larger-Print novels and my 2 FREE mystery gifts (gifts worth about $10). After receiving them, if I don't wish to receive any more books, I can return the shipping statement marked "cancel." If I don't cancel, I will receive 4 brand-new larger-print novels every month and be billed just $4.99 per book in the U.S. or $5.74 per book in Canada. That's a savings of at least 23% off the cover price. It's quite a bargain! Shipping and handling is just 50¢ per book in the U.S. and 75¢ per book in Canada.* I understand that accepting the 2 free books and gifts places me under no obligation to buy anything. I can always return a shipment and cancel at any time. Even if I never buy another book, the two free books and gifts are mine to keep forever.

161/361 IDN F47N

Name _____ (PLEASE PRINT)

Address _____ Apt. #

City _____ State/Prov. _____ Zip/Postal Code

Signature (if under 18, a parent or guardian must sign)

Mail to the Harlequin® Reader Service:
IN U.S.A.: P.O. Box 1867, Buffalo, NY 14240-1867
IN CANADA: P.O. Box 609, Fort Erie, Ontario L2A 5X3

* Terms and prices subject to change without notice. Prices do not include applicable taxes. Sales tax applicable in N.Y. Canadian residents will be charged applicable taxes. Offer not valid in Quebec. This offer is limited to one order per household. Not valid for current subscribers to Harlequin Heartwarming larger-print books. All orders subject to credit approval. Credit or debit balances in a customer's account(s) may be offset by any other outstanding balance owed by or to the customer. Please allow 4 to 6 weeks for delivery. Offer available while quantities last.

Your Privacy—The Harlequin® Reader Service is committed to protecting your privacy. Our Privacy Policy is available online at www.ReaderService.com or upon request from the Harlequin Reader Service.

We make a portion of our mailing list available to reputable third parties that offer products we believe may interest you. If you prefer that we not exchange your name with third parties, or if you wish to clarify or modify your communication preferences, please visit us at www.ReaderService.com/consumerschoice or write to us at Harlequin Reader Service Preference Service, P.O. Box 9062, Buffalo, NY 14269. Include your complete name and address.

HWDIR13R